New Girl
and Other Stories of Teen Life

New Girl
and Other Stories of Teen Life

Selected by Miriam Goldberger

SCHOLASTIC BOOK SERVICES
New York Toronto London Auckland Sydney Tokyo

For reprint permission, grateful acknowledgment is made to:

AMERICAN GIRL Magazine and the author for 'Merry Christmas, Mary Catherine" by Estelle Bamberg from the December 1970 issue of AMERICAN GIRL Magazine.

Curtis Brown Ltd. for "The Onlooker" by Elizabeth Allen, copyright © 1970 by Dell Publishing Company, Inc. First appeared in INGENUE.

John Cushman Associates, Inc. for "My Grandpa's Lump of Five Wasted Years" by William Vincent Burgess, copyright © 1970 by William Vincent Burgess.

Joan Dash for "The Cover-Up". Reprinted from SEVENTEEN, copyright © 1968 by Triangle Publications, Inc.

E.P. Dutton & Co., Inc. for "New Girl" by Elizabeth Allen from "YOU CAN'T SAY WHAT YOU THINK AND OTHER STORIES," copyright © 1968, 1962, 1961, 1959 by Elizabeth Allen.

Susan Ingalls for "The Ideal Couple". Reprinted from SEVENTEEN, copyright © 1969 by Triangle Publications, Inc.

INGENUE Magazine for "A Memory of Butterflies" by Thomaline Aguallo. Reprinted from INGENUE (August 1969) with the permission of the Dell Publishing Company.

E. A. Proulx for "The Baroque Marble". Reprinted from SEVENTEEN, copyright © 1970 by Triangle Publications, Inc.

TEEN Magazine for "After All, We're Both Aquarians" by Elizabeth Allen (February 1971);
"Charlie Brown Would Understand" by Thomaline Aguallo (September 1969);
"Forever Christmas" by Joel Locksely (December 1970);
"The Girl Who Talked to Frogs" by Thomaline Aguallo Buchan (June 1971);
"My Own Thing" by Audrey Lazier (August 1969);
"The Robin Game" by Ruth Pinter (April 1971);
"The Rolling Scones—A Colossal Catering Caper" by James William Dugel (February 1971);
"The Street Where My Heart Lives" by Ellen Schafter Conrad (March 1971);
"Which is the Way to Where" by Pat Lawler (May 1971).

CONTENTS

CHARLIE BROWN WOULD UNDERSTAND

THOMALINE AGUALLO

I didn't have a fantastic figure or a fabulous face. I didn't even want him, so what could Handsome Harvey Whipple want with me?

In the first place, I have always liked to think of myself as a "Champion of the Underdog." (My mother says that what I *really* mean is I'm a sucker, but my mother has no *soul*.)

At any rate, to understand fully how I got myself into this — uh — predicament, you must bear in mind that I, Bridget Bishop, have always been a su — that is, I have always been sympathetic to unfortunate situations. Is there a lost child wandering around a department store? It's probably *my* shoulder he'll cry his sticky ice-cream tears on. Is there someone collecting funds for the Save the Blue-Eyed Duckbilled-Platypus from Extinction? He'll get all my pimple cream money for *this* week.

7

Do you need someone to cry over your spilled milk, lost dog, stolen love, et cetera, et cetera? Then slosh your way over to my house and wade on up to my room. You'll probably find me weeping copiously over a vivid account of someone's Uncle Herbert, who was imprisoned (falsely) for 32 years on trumped-up pornographic comic-book charges. (You can see that my mercy is boundless.)

And so you can see too that I have a gentle, compassionate nature. (My brother William suggests that I change that to *mushy empty-headedness*. I in turn have suggested that William turn his brilliant, evil little mind back to thoughts of dissecting little old ladies, or whatever it is that he does in his room.) Anyway, my gentle nature (or whatever) has always influenced me in affairs of the heart.

Someone I greatly admire once said, "There's nothing like unrequited love to ruin the taste of a peanut butter sandwich." Oh, how true. I myself have waded through veritable mountains of tasteless peanut butter sandwiches searching for *my* one true love.

My mother (who is, in addition to being very short, a super bread baker and the World's Most Misunderstood Sculptor, also the greatest dispenser of free — and unwanted — advice) has often suggested to me that were it she, she might have picked someone a little more suave for a love idol. (Only politeness and true devotion prevent me from mentioning then that my father, whom I love dearly, isn't likely to be mistaken for Cary Grant.)

And anyway, I really don't care what she thinks. I only know what my heart tells me, and my heart

8

tells me that the man of my dreams will very likely resemble the lovably bumbling wide-mouthed little clown who made the famous peanut butter quote above.

That's right: I'm madly in love with Charlie Brown.

I can't help it. It happened when I waited faithfully for what seemed like weeks while the whole world trembled, and we all wondered whether he was *really* going to drop that baseball. And when he did, they all yelled "YOU BLOCKHEAD, CHARLIE BROWN!"

Well, when his head drooped — *my* head dropped. When his mouth quivered, *my* mouth quivered. William called it an orgy of self-pity.

I called it love.

Naturally, one cannot hope ever to marry a cartoon. And besides, what I really wanted most was a real life Charlie Brown of my own: some well-intentioned young man who would stumble through life with me. Together we would take the weight of the world on our weary young shoulders; together we would say exactly the wrong thing to exactly the right person; together . . . well, you see what I mean. Let the other girls sigh hugely over their Paul Newmans and Paul McCartneys—let them even give a little giggle over their Frank Zappas. I *knew* what I wanted.

And it was with typical Charlie Brown luck that I almost didn't get it. Because when Handsome Harvey Whipple, Most Beautiful Boy in School, chose to fall in love, did he select Sally Carver, of the fabulous figure, or Tiffany (born Martha) Monroe, of the fantastic face?

He did not. Instead he selected a five-foot-two, nearsighted, barefoot kook — your little old story-teller, me.

I know how goofy that must sound. Usually in stories like these, it's a case of poor-goony-girl-has-a-fantastic-crush-on-handsome-school-hero-boy. Then follows two- or three-thousand words of how she pines away for him until that fateful day he discovers that if she takes off her glasses and lets down her hair — *voila!* — she's a perfect *double* for Julie Christie (or Katharine Ross, or whoever else happens to be in vogue at the moment. Not so in my case. No taking off of glasses (which I'm too vain to wear anyway) will change my looks. I am forever fated to go through life as a round, blonde girl — in other words, a *female* Charlie Brown looking for her mate.

I remember the way it started. It was a fine sunny day and all of us were sitting in Mrs. Blank-enburg's Spanish III class. We were all listening to Mrs. (or *Señora*) Blankenburg order a three-course meal in Spanish. Señora Blankenburg had chosen to wear for this occasion her daring green-purple-and-pink *sarape*, her Tijuana *huaraches* (which squeaked everytime she breathed), and a slightly wilted rose behind her ear.

I was barely aware of the Señora's voice as it plodded its way through a remarkably dreary din-ner of avocado soup, fried chicken, cottage cheese, and something that sounded like a fried bean sun-dae for dessert, although I'm probably mistaken about that last item. (I probably *am* wrong about that; I had just finished ordering what I thought was a tasty meal and then found out it consisted of three teacups, a bowl of soap, an orange, and a doorknob for dessert. But at least *I* wouldn't go into a Mexican restaurant and order fried chicken!)

So, having decided to stick to American menus for awhile, I was sneaking a look at a *Peanuts* paperback I just happened to uncover under a pile of my brother William's underwear, when a note suddenly slid down the middle of the book, mercifully obliterating another great Lucy-putdown of my poor Charlie Brown.

"*Querida,*" the note said (and it took me a minute to realize that it meant "darling," and not flat tire, or something), "sitting here watching you while trying to listen to old Bat-knees Blankenburg is driving me mad. . . ." Well, at that point I had of course decided that this little love letter was definitely not for me. Perhaps I was supposed to pass it on to someone. I looked around for Sally or Tiffany-Martha, or even Imogene Brown, who was cross-eyed but amply endowed elsewhere. But none of those class beauties were located anywhere near me. There was only Pimples McGowan, class bully, and Hajii Bagamandabarian, our foreign exchange student, in front and in back of me. Pimples was snoring loudly and Hajii was consuming the last of his daily pound of Armenian cheese, and both seemed less than desirable at that moment. So I shrugged and read on.

". . . driving me mad," it continued, "I love to watch you bite your nails down to the quick. I love the way you scratch the dandruff from behind your ear. I love all the juicy round blondeness of you. Please say you'll meet me after school by the birdbath. Love, Harvey."

I gasped audibly and then looked wildly around the room for Harvey. When I found him, he was

11

staring angelically up at Señora Blankenburg. "Perhaps," she sniffed, "Señorita Bishop would like to tell us the word for swivel-headed."

"Uh, n-no," I stammered, clutching the note in my hot little hand, my insides crumbling at the thought of the Señora finding the piece of paper and — horror of horrors — reading it out loud to the class. (She's had it in for me since the time she came to dinner at my house and was served one of my mother's specialties — burned baked potatoes, lemon soup, and three chapters of my father's latest unintelligible novel.)

Mercifully, the bell rang. I tried to fight my way over to Harvey to find out the purpose of this joke — it could only *be* a joke, and I wanted no part of it. But he was gone, swept away in a tide of adoring teeny-boppers, their little hearts thumping, their carefully blushered cheeks blushing ever redder at the thought of being next to one who was reported to be so suave he even wore a paisley scarf when he worked on his car.

Well, there was nothing to do then but wait and go to my next — and last — class and try to decide whether to keep that date by the birdbath.

Twenty minutes later, dressed in my rumpled gym shorts and blouse (my mother spent last weekend in spiritual meditation; *I* understand, but try and explain to your gym teacher!), I consulted with my best friend, Angie Carlucci, as we hid behind a bush trying to avoid being captured and made to play Healthful and Recreational Games.

"What do you think?" I asked, shoving the note at her. She adjusted the rim of her outsized sunglasses.

"Well," she said, taking a bite of contraband banana. (Angie is five feet seven and weighs approximately 22 pounds. She eats like a horse and I, who gain 10 pounds looking at advertisements, hate her.) "Well," she said again, "Well."

"Is that all you're going to say?" I demanded. "I might as well ask William for advice, for heaven's sake! Or my mother!"

Her head shot up. "Good lord," she murmured through a mouthful of banana. "Imagine your mother giving you romantic advice."

We both contemplated the terrible thought.

"But do you think it's a joke?" I asked then. "And if it is, why? And if it *isn't*, why?"

She shook her head. "I'm just really not sure," she said. "Somehow I just can't conjure up a picture of you and Handsome Harvey doing one of those swank dinners of his." We both knew the legend of Harvey and his superduper dates. They began with his picking you up in his low, sleek, red MG, continued through dinner at an intimate little French place (complete with wine, some said), and ended with a smooth drive down the coast, Harvey's beautiful profile glistening in the dark, the seductive guitar sounds of his eight-track stereo tape playing quietly around you. . . . Sigh!

Well, it might sound like a bit much to you, but when you consider that most of the young men around town feel that a hamburger, an Orange Julius, and an evening spent listening to *your* records is spoiling you, well. . .

On the other hand, Harvey has always seemed a bit much to *me*. I've never been able to get along with perfection, and Harvey Whipple was as near to perfection as I was liable to get. Six feet two, thick black hair curling gracefully down the back

13

of his neck, clear blue eyes, and an athletic body which seemed to be able to perform superbly any task he required of it. He moved lithe and catlike through the halls, his shirts clean and bright, his shoes always shined, his neck always clean. He never said much; he just smiled his radiant perfect snow-white smile, and women — old and young alike — melted into great lump of quivering flesh.

All except me. I know who I am. I know that things will invariably go just a little wrong for me, that I'll probably say the wrong thing at the proper time, that glasses have a habit of slipping from my hand, that my nylons always manage to have just a little bit of a run. And I'm still happy. I don't mind that I'll never sail smoothly through life but just sort of stumble around instead. I guess that's what attracted me to Charlie Brown in the first place; the troubles of the world surround him, the Lucys of the world berate him, the Great Pumpkin ignores him, and his dog has a better personality than he does. But he doesn't care. He knows who he is too. Oh, it's a Charlie Brown I'm after, not a Handsome Harvey!

But knowing who I was still didn't answer my question for me. "Should I meet Harvey or not?" I asked Angie, but she was at that moment being dragged off by the volleyball team and could not tell me.

Warily I made my way along the cobbled path. Ahead of me in the far-off distance was the town birdbath, mysteriously devoid of its usual crowd of dogs, cats, gangs of little boys, mothers pushing babies in strollers — in short, most of the town. (About three years ago the birds gave up in disgust, abandoned the birdbath to the local populace, and commenced bathing in the park water fountain.)

Curiosity had consumed me, and I could not help passing by after school to see if Harvey showed up. I still couldn't figure out why he wanted to see me. Maybe it was a new club initiation — see who can get dopey old Bridget to walk by the birthbath. There were probably 50 million people all cleverly concealed behind lampposts waiting to see me make a fool of myself. On the other hand . . .

I wasn't long in finding out the answer. As I walked the last few steps to the birdbath, a racy red MG zipped up in front of me and Mr. Suave himself leaned over and flung open the door.

"Hop in," he said.

"My mother told me always to keep my skirts down, my legs crossed," I said primly, "and never to accept rides from strangers."

He sighed. "Bridget," he said, "your skirts — when you wear skirts — are too short to be kept down; you sit like a football player, and I've known you since we were five years old and in kindergarten together."

"You got me there," I agreed and got in. "So, Harvey. What's it all about, then?"

"What's what all about?" he asked, all innocence and wide blue-eyed stare.

"YOU know," I said. "All this mushy note business. If you need money, I'm in debt to my brother William for about a million dollars. If you want to copy my homework, please remember I'm the girl who orders doorknobs — and that's about all I can think you'd want *me* for."

"What about," he whispered, "love?"

"Excuse me, Harvey, I didn't hear you."

"Love," he whispered again.

"What?"

"LOVE!" he shouted, raising the top of his car by two inches.

"Oh, yeah," I said, "that. Did you want me to get you someone's phone number?"

"Yes," he said, gritting his teeth. "Yours."

"Oh, Harvey," I said, "don't be silly. Why would you want to call me? Anyway, we don't have a telephone. My father says it's just industry's way of trying to capture his soul."

He sat silently, his head drooping over the steering wheel. *That's it.* I thought, *he has blackouts. He was having one when he wrote that note.* I flipped back through my memories — gym class — first aid — blackouts — nothing. *It's too bad,* I thought sadly, *he doesn't have a broken leg.*

Then he turned his liquid gaze on me. He took several deep breaths. "Bridget," he said finally, "I love you."

"Harvey," I said kindly, "don't worry about it. You're just losing your mind. Let me do something for you. Would you like me to break your leg?"

He pounded his fists on the steering wheel. "What's the matter with you?" he screamed. "I, Handsome Harvey Whipple, have just declared undying love for you, Bridget Bishop, a nice, but (you will excuse the expression) rather nothing of a girl."

"I excuse the expression," I said. "But if that's the way you feel, how can you possibly think you love me? I mean, according to you, I hardly deserve you."

He nodded matter-of-factly. "Mmmm, that's very

true. You really don't. I don't know, Bridge. I can't explain it. I mean, for instance, when I take Sally Carver out, well, we both look great, and we go have a nice dinner, and then we take a drive and then, well, that's it. Like, we can't do anything else because she'll get her hair messed or her dress wrinkled or my car dirty or my shoes scuffed. And we have to go someplace where people can see us because that seems to be about the only thing that holds us together. I mean, we honestly spend all night talking about what people are saying about us. . . . 'My, what a handsome couple' and all that junk. Blah," he snorted in disgust. "But *you*, well, you wouldn't mind going to the beach on a windy day, or cooking hot dogs over an open fire. And you say what you want, even if it comes out dumb —"

Charlie Brown again. "Thanks," I said grimly.

" — and, I don't know, you are who you are, and I think maybe you're the most content person I know."

"But is that love?" I said.

"Oh," he said, "you mean birds singing and bells ringing la, la?"

"Well, yes," I admitted, "I had sort of hoped that when someone ever happened to mention love to me, there might be a little chirp or two thrown in. Good for the ego, you know."

"But, Bridget," he said wonderingly, "you don't *have* an ego!"

I stared in amazement. Was it true? Was that the key to Charlie Brown and me? Did we just accept the things in our lives as just that — things in our lives and nothing more or less — and goodbye to yesterday and hello, tomorrow?

I looked at Harvey. This desirable (according

to rumor) young man, admired by one and all, was offering his magnificent self to me, Bridget Bishop, at whom most people just smiled vaguely and patted kindly while they went on their ambitious ways. By all rights, I should consider myself properly humiliated, gather up my tattered notebook, and silently steal away. . . .

But no. Suddenly I saw this moment in its true light. This was the baseball that wouldn't come down. This was the latest rejection from the little girls with their curly hair. This was Lucy's birthday party to which he was again not invited.

It was Charlie Brown's revenge.

I held out my hand grandly. "Okay, Harvey," I said, "if you love me, you love me. It's a groove."

A look of relief spread across his flawless face. "Let's celebrate," he said, starting his (our) car. "Let's go buy SuperSurfer Sundaes. I don't even care if you spill chocolate sauce on your blouse."

Plop. The baseball landed squarely in Charlie Brown's glove.

"The whole thing," I said cheerfully, "will probably wind up in your lap."

Perhaps another time I would meet my true stumbling soul mate. Perhaps Harvey underneath all that perfection was a bumbler too. It didn't matter, though. The only thing that mattered was enjoying the fruit of a victory I hadn't even wanted to win.

Charlie Brown, I knew, would be the first to understand.

MERRY CHRISTMAS, MARY CATHERINE

ESTELLE G. BAMBERG

It's obvious to Mary Catherine that she is no longer a child. Is everyone else unaware of the truth?

To think she had been so thrilled — thrilled to muteness beyond even a simple "thank you" — when Johnny Raulton gave her the Christmas present!

That he should have noticed her at all was enough to make her nearly drop to the floor. He was her brother Leslie's friend. Before, although she had known him most of her life, he seldom said anything to her except, "Hi there, Mary Catherine." His eyes were the color of maple syrup. He was long and rangy, the quiet type, with an easy, catchy kind of smile.

For as long as she could remember, all of Mary Catherine's daydreams had been concentrated on Johnny.

What a moron she must have seemed, then, speechless with surprise while the stain of shyness heated and reddened in her face, the excitement in her rising so fast she could have floated right out of herself. For ages she'd kept standing there like a dummy, staring up into his eyes as if she'd lost her mind or something. Mortification, like fever, burned in her face at the thought of it now.

Still, for an instant, it had seemed to Mary Catherine that Johnny too had been locked in that magical, magnetic moment. But then her brother Leslie had come into the living room with his coat slung over his shoulders, and Johnny said, "Ready, Les? Good, let's go!"

They had dates. With whom, Mary Catherine didn't know. Leslie was nineteen, Johnny was eighteen. Their girl friends (there was a seemingly endless supply) were objects of Mary Catherine's unstinting envy. Impartially and equally, and with passion, Mary Catherine wished them all stricken with acne and baldness. It would be *years* before she could compete with them. She knew that. . . .

For a moment, with Johnnny's present in her hands and his eyes on hers, she'd thought that finally, finally he'd realized she was no longer a child. He had turned to her even as Les was urging him through the door, and, nodding at his gift to her, said, "When I saw it in the store I immediately thought of you, Mary Catherine." She had actually trembled with delight.

"Nut head!" Mary Catherine moaned now. "Stupid nut head!" Applying the epithet to Johnny as well, she rolled on her bed from her back to her stomach and buried her face in the pillow.

What was wrong with him, anyway? Couldn't he see what a terrific insult his gift was to someone as old as fourteen? Oh, she might have known! No matter how old she got to be, Johnny would never see her as anything more than Leslie's *kid* sister.

She didn't care how pretty the doll was. Its luxurious fall of brown hair could have been the cascading snakes of Medusa's head; its lustrous, green-flecked eyes couldn't have been more despised. A toy. For a child. She flung the doll — and its wrapping — to the floor. It had robbed all the *merry* from this Christmas.

Mary Catherine raised her head from the pillow and peered morosely at the floor.

The doll, one leg twisted beneath it, stared, stiff-lashed and unblinking, back at her. A card bearing Johnny's looping signature was crumpled beside it. Above his name he had written: "When I bring you this doll, little girl, I am reminded of the coming of spring: bright, clear air, and the first scent of flowers."

Little girl. Those two words leaped out at her. "Little girl!" she muttered grimly. Soon she would be a creaky old maid, and he'd probably go right on treating her as though she were still in a stroller. Years from now he would probably . . .

A horrible thought came and shook her to the quick. Years from now, Johnny's collection of girls would certainly have gotten down to only one. Mary Catherine could see her. A phony, over made-up thing, but glamorous and dazzlingly blonde.

Oh, you could just bet Johnny would never give that girl a doll!

Cumulative tears trickled slowly from Mary

21

Catherine's eyes. It would have been better if Johnny hadn't given her anything at all.

Swiping bleakly at her eyes and suddenly tired now, she got out of bed and took her pajamas down from the hook. Undressing slowly, she got into them.

It was still early, but all she wanted to do now was to go to sleep and forget about Johnny Raulton. Lying in the dark with her dreams in shattered fragments around her, she made up her mind: From now on, whenever he came to the house, she would simply say, "Hi," and go into another room.

Never again would she look at him long enough to let him read in her eyes the feeling she had for him. Even if he tried to detain her, she would keep her cool and tell him she was sorry, but she was too busy to talk. Let him blow his mind on that for awhile!

Just as she was stretching into sleepfulness, the telephone rang.

It rang again, that shrill, compelling instrument, and though Mary Catherine wasn't up to rapping with any of her friends tonight, she popped to a sitting position and grabbed up the receiver.

"Hello?"

"Mary Catherine?"

She pushed thick strands of brown hair back from her brow. The voice was Johnny's. "Yes," she said.

For a moment there was nothing but his breathing and the thin hum of the wire. Then, all in a rush, he said, "I just wanted to know if you liked my present — and the message on the card?"

As usually happened whenever Johnny spoke to

her, Mary Catherine's tongue turned to cotton. "The — uh — message?"

"Didn't you read it?" he asked. As if to belie the seriousness behind his words, he gave a brief little chuckle. "I composed it. It was meant as a tribute."

"Oh!" It came out half-sigh, half-snort, and Mary Catherine felt so dumb she could have kicked herself. "Oh," she repeated louder this time, "did you really write it yourself?"

"That's what I said." He gave another chuckle. "I mean — the doll — it inspired me, and . . ."

"I know, you told me." She made a wry face, "When you saw it in the store you thought of me."

"Well — it wasn't that I *thought* of you so much as that I was *reminded* of you."

Mary Catherine's green-flecked, hazel eyes widened. There was a subtle distinction between *a thought of someone* and *being reminded of her*.

As she was about to ask for clarification, there came an insistent knocking in the background; Johnny, his voice turning abruptly hurried, said, "We're in the theatre, and the movie just broke. Les is pounding on the phone booth. Just a sec — "

He evidently opened the door of the booth, for immediately she heard Les and the girls piling in on him, and a babble of good-natured voices overriding his protests.

"OK," Johnny conceded to them. "Just let me say good-bye." Into the phone he said quickly, "I've got to go or they'll drag me out. But, listen —" his voice dropped, "— in case I didn't wish you one before, Merry Christmas, Mary Catherine."

For a long moment she just sat there with the phone in her hand. Then, she whispered "Merry

23

Christmas" into it, and replaced the receiver, setting it softly onto its base.

With her mouth parted in a slight smile, she got up and took a step over to where the doll and card still lay. She picked up the doll and studied it, seeing, for the first time, its unmistakable likeness to herself. She bent and retrieved the card.

And, as she stood there, cradling the doll tenderly in her arms, the woman who had sprung into being inside her watched and smiled and was content to wait.

THE BAROQUE MARBLE

E. A. PROULX

Sister Opal's dream almost comes true, but is almost enough?

Late autumn rain again. Sister Opal woke up in a
Polaroid yellow light with her head hanging off
the bed sideways. Down in the street children's
voices slid under the window muffled and changed
by the damp morning. Sister Opal thought the
children sounded as if they were speaking Russian
or Basque — some queer, garbled language. She
pretended she was in another country where she
didn't know a word of the language and where she
would have to make signs to get breakfast in a few
minutes when she went downstairs. False panic began to rise in her, then subsided. From her position
of supension over the edge of the bed, the furniture
looked darker, and the unfamiliar angle gave it a
sinister look. The bureau loomed, a skyscraper in

25

dull, dark varnish. Perhaps there were tiny people and offices inside. The chair arms seemed to have clenched hands at their ends, like brown old men sitting anxiously in the doctor's office waiting to hear the bad news.

Sister Opal twisted her head around toward the yellow window. On the sill was a square glass jar of marbles: reddish brown, yellow, and white glassies, and a very large blue one. Most of them were mob marbles, as much alike as the faces of the crowd to a dictator on his balcony. Off to one side of the jar there was a white marble, deformed and not a true round — a lopsided freak of a marble — her favorite one. When this marble sat alone on the splendor of Sister Opal's blue velvet best dress, it took on a silver, translucent glow. In the jar, it was dirty-white, opaque, and with more space around it than the other marbles, as if they avoided getting too close to it.

The jar of marbles was a kind of wealth. It was the most Sister Opal owned. Eight hundred and forty-three marbles. She took a miser's satisfaction in pouring them out onto the bed, watching them roll into the valleys the sheets made, gathering up their heavy, glassy weight, cold but soon warming in her hand. Each marble was individually beautiful. A kind of classic Greek perfection shone in their roundness. Under Sister Opal's father's magnifying glass the perfect marbles disclosed blemishes, pits, and scratches. Sister Opal liked them unmagnified; in their smallness she found their greatest value.

She touched the shade and it leaped up, startled, to the top of the wooden roller where it chattered a few seconds in fright, and then clung, tightly wound. Her warm breath made a milky fog on the window glass and her finger wrote, "All the sailors have died of scurvy, yours truly, Opal Foote."

In another room, Sister Opal's family sat at the table. Dark and sullen, they crunched toast, stabbed at their eggs, and made whirlpools in their coffee with spoons. Except for Sister Opal, it was a bad-tempered family in the mornings and the only coversations were mumbles to each other to pass the sugar or salt. By noontime the family would be chatty and warm, and by suppertime everyone was in high spirits. Sister Opal's four brothers (except for Roy, who worked on the night shift at G.E.) were very jovial at suppertime when Sister Opal was weary. This morning Sister Opal's father asked about homework. Sister Opal thought of homework as yellow leaves dropping softly down, like the yellow blank pages she had dropped into the wastepaper basket last night. Guilty, Sister Opal went outside with jammy toast, hearing something from her father about being home right after school to make up Roy's dinner pail and to start supper because Mama had to work late. Sister Opal sang a private song as she walked along the wet sidewalk hopping the shallow puddles which were out to ruin her good shoes.

> *Sailors died of scurvy, oh,*
> *They threw them in the sea.*
> *Pack Roy's dinner pail tonight*
> *With a thermos bottle of tea.*

The rain outside had transmuted to yellow light and threatened afternoon lightning. Somewhere

Sister Opal had read that yellow was the favorite color of insane people. The woman down the street had had a nervous breakdown last summer only a week after her husband had painted their house yellow. Across the street some white boys from Sister Opal's class at school were walking in the same direction. They pushed and shoved each other. One of them yelled, "Hey, turkey!" at Sister Opal. Sister Opal laughed because their faces looked yellow. Immediately they became hostile, thinking she was laughing at their existence, their being. Sister Opal's dignity did not allow her to hear their jeers.

At three-thirty Sister Opal was not on her way back home to pack up Roy's dinner pail. Instead, she was walking thoughtfully down Essex Street, peering into all the windows of the silver and antique shops. Art class that afternoon had completely enthralled Sister Opal. Mrs. Grigson had shown a film about ordinary people who started art collections with inexpensive things that became rare and valuable as time went by. Sister Opal envisioned herself someday in her own apartment with rare *objets d'art* in glass cases and white walls hung with glowing works of great artists which she, Sister Opal, had picked up years before for just a song. Even though she had only a few dollars (a birthday present from her grandmother), in her savings account and little hope of getting more, she was looking for something really good and fine on Essex Street. The film had indicated that all the people who built up enviable art collections had started off with the things they really liked. This was Sister Opal's primary mission: to find something she really liked. Then she would face the money problem. She had quite forgotten about Roy's empty dinner pail, the cold stove, and Mama working late.

As she splashed through the puddles of Essex Street, she dismissed old silver, all lumpy with twisted roses and crests, and dark with tarnish. She rejected the idea of collecting glass — too space-consuming and bothersome. She didn't really like sculpture, and she didn't know where she could buy real paintings or prints. The rain began again and Sister Opal's shoes were sodden and squishy. Past shops with small, dirty windows she went, discarding ceramics, carved wooden figures, *épergnes*, *demilunes*, vases, chandeliers, toy soldiers, *netsuke*, andirons, do-grates. Meissen, Tung horses, lacquerware, and crystal.

Then, in the window of R. Sonnier's, she saw *it*. On a piece of blue velvet, quite like Sister Opal's best dress, there lay a large, glowing, misshapen marble. Sister Opal drew in her breath and exhaled slowly. This was it. She would collect marbles, rare ones from China, ancient ones from Peru, Roman marbles, marbles Ghenghis Khan had played with, marbles from Napoleon's cabinets, from Istanbul and Alexandria, marbles of solid gold, of azure, of lapis lazuli, of wood and stone and jewel. And she would begin with the marble in this very window! In she marched, a thin black girl with wet shoes, whose older brother was going to go supperless on the night shift.

The shop inside was crowded with objects stacked on shelves, in corners, or looming down from the ceiling, crumpled, dusty, dark things. A fat, middle-aged white man was sitting in a leather chair be-

29

hind the counter and reading a book. He looked up when the door opened and then back to his book. Sister Opal did not waste time looking around the shop. She marched briskly up to R. Sonnier, or as briskly as one can march with wet shoes.

"Excuse me, how much is that marble in the window, and do you have any other kinds?"

"*What* marble in the window? I haven't got any marble that I know of in there. This is an antique shop, not a toy store." Sister Opal went to the curtain that hung behind the window to give a background for the objects displayed and pulled it aside.

"There," she said simply, pointing to the fat, lucent sphere.

"Young lady," said R. Sonnier, highly amused. "that is *not* a marble. That is a baroque pearl, an antique baroque pearl, and even though I am letting it go at an unbelievably low price, I doubt you could afford it." He looked her up and down, seeing the wet shoes, the cotton dress in late October, the brown skin, and thinness that was Sister Opal. "It is for sale for four hundred and fifty dollars. A bargain for those who can afford such things. Marbles I believe you'll find at Woolworth's."

Sister Opal felt a horrible combination of shame, embarrassment, anger, pride, and sadness rise in her. She carried as a memory for the rest of her life R. Sonnier's knowing look that dismissed her as a person of no importance at all. Sister Opal, in a burst of pride and fantasy, said in a haughty voice, "*I* prefer to think of baroque pearls as marbles. And I would definitely like *that* marble.

Please save it for me because it might be quite awhile before I can pick it up. My name is Opal Foote."

R. Sonnier digested this information and repeated, "Then you want me to save this baroque pearl for you? You intend to buy it?"

"Yes," said Sister Opal. "Opal Foote is the name." She gave him her address and then left with her shoes squelching softly. She was committed to the baroque marble which R. Sonnier was saving for her. Suddenly she remembered Roy's dinner pail and the gloomy apartment without one picture or really nice thing in it. There were only the family photographs kept in an old candy box and a plastic vase filled with plastic flowers. She ran home hoping that Roy hadn't left for work yet.

At the table that night Sister Opal's father looked on her with disfavor. His cheerful supper face was cloudy, and Sister Opal knew the storm would break before she poured out his coffee. Roy had had to go to work without any dinner, supper had been late, and Opal had broken three eggs by slamming the old refrigerator door so hard that the eggs had shot out of their aluminum nest and run all over everything inside. Sister Opal's father finished the last bit of mashed potato on his plate and leaned back, glaring at Sister Opal.

"Well, girl, how come you didn't get home to fix your brother's dinner pail or start the supper? Everybody in this family's got to do his part. Now I'm waiting to hear."

There was no escape. Sister Opal took a deep breath and began telling about the art class and

Essex Street and the baroque pearl in R. Sonnier's shop. Her father's face was first incredulous, then angry, then sad. He said nothing for a long time. Opal sat miserably waiting for the lecture. Her brother Andrew got up and poured the coffee and patted Opal's shoulder as he passed behind her chair. Her father began to speak, slowly at first.

"Well, Sister, I think for a family in the kind of situation we got, where we all work to keep some kind of decency in our lives, and where we are trying to work toward an education for all you kids, an education of *some* kind, that any ideas about collecting art are just plain *crazy*. We are poor people and it's no use you pretending otherwise. Maybe someday your children, or more likely, grandchildren can collect art, but right now, Girl, we can't gather enough money together to collect milk bottles! Wait!" (Sister Opal had uttered a furious "But!")

"Now just wait! I don't want to crush you down like a pancake. I *know* how you felt when that antique man looked you up and down and made his remarks. Every person in this family knows how you felt. And I understand how you answered him back pridefully about how you'd *get* that pearl or marble or whatever it is. But now, Opal, you got to swallow your pride and forget that marble, or else you got to do something about it. You got any ideas? Because I personally do not."

"I am old enough and able enough to get a job after school in the evenings and earn enough money to *buy* that baroque pearl myself, and I am going to do it!" Opal spoke slowly.

Her father looked at Opal, sadder than ever, and

said, "If you are old enough to get a job, Sister Opal, you are old enough to save that job money for college or for helping this big family to get along. How would it be if I decided to save the money I make at Quadrant for buying myself a Picasso or something? Or suppose Roy decided not to kick in money for groceries and things but to buy himself a — a — harpsichord or a statue?" The idea of big, quiet Roy, clumsy and inarticulate, buying himself a harpsichord or a statue sent half the table snorting with laughter. "Besides," continued her father, "who's going to pack up Roy's dinner pail and start the supper while you are at some job?"

Sister Opal's brother Andrew stood up. "I am sick and tired of hearing about Roy's dinner pail. I expect the sun isn't going to come up and set anymore — no, it's going to be Roy's dinner pail! I say that if Sister Opal sees more in life than groceries and trying to get along, she should at least have the chance to try. I can get home a little earlier and start supper myself, and Roy can pack up his *own* dinner pail. You've told us yourself, Papa, that if a person wants something bad enough, and works hard enough *for* it, he'll get it. I'm willing to see Opal get that baroque pearl. I wouldn't mind seeing a few nice things around here myself."

A great argument broke out and raged around the supper table and took on fresh vigor when Sister Opal's mother came in, tired and with a sharp edge to her tongue. The final resolution, near midnight, was that if Sister Opal got a job, she could save half the money for the baroque pearl and half for college. Sister Opal felt triumphant and like a real art collector.

It took her three days to find a job. She was to work at Edsall's drugstore after school until ten-thirty from Monday to Friday and all day Saturday. She dipped out ice cream, made sodas and cherry Cokes, mixed Alka-Seltzer for gray-faced men, sold cigars and newspapers, squeezed her homework in between customers, and wiped off the sticky counter with a yellow sponge (Mr. Edsall had bought five hundred yellow sponges at a bargain sale the year before and Sister Opal got to despise those yellow sponges). She made change for people to use in the phone booth; she cleaned out the Pyrex coffeepots, and made fresh coffee a thousand times a day, sold cough drops and throat lozenges all through the winter, and dispensed little plastic hats to ladies when the spring rains came. She got home at eleven o'clock each night with aching legs and red eyes, and Sunday mornings she slept late, catching up. In little ways, her mother showed an extra tenderness for her only daughter's great desire for a beautiful object. Her father surprised Sister Opal by Scotch-taping a reproduction of a Picasso painting over the kitchen calendar. He had cut *The Three Musicians* out of an old magazine. When Roy said, "What's that!?" Sister Opal's father remarked loftily, "I always did like Picasso."

"Yeah," said Andrew to Roy, "at least he doesn't go in for harpsichords and statues." This joke about harpsichords and statues was one that Roy had never quite fathomed, and he eventually grew so confused on the matter that he was convinced that he really did take an extraordinary interest in key-board music and sculpture. It was even suspected by the family that on his night off he had once gone, not to a night baseball game, but to a concert.

Sister Opal's weeks turned into months, and the long drugstore nights dragged through winter into spring. She had two bank accounts, one for college money and one for the baroque pearl. In March on a Friday night, she had four hundred dollars in the school account, and four hundred fifty in the pearl account. It was enough. She got permission from Mr. Edsall to take the next day off to go to R. Sonnier's to buy the pearl.

Early in the morning Sister Opal woke to a pale yellow spring sun. She leaped up with her heart beating hard and dressed the part of a baroque pearl-buyer. Something special was needed. Her blue velvet best dress had been outgrown and re-made during the winter into a blue velvet best skirt. She put it on and borrowed her mother's white silk blouse. She shined her shoes until the cracks didn't show and rush in to breakfast. Everybody knew she was going to buy the pearl that day but nobody said anything. The whole family was shy and still with anticipation. Andrew sat breathing quietly on his coffee.

At nine o'clock Sister Opal was walking along Essex Street. She went past the dusty windows displaying lumpy silverware, ceramic mugs with gold decorations, wooden candelabra from Spain, and then she came to R. Sonnier's shop. In his window there was a display of silver and gold watches and clocks under glass bells. Sister Opal smiled, think-

35

ing of the baroque pearl hidden secretly in a box, waiting for Sister Opal all those long months. She went inside. R. Sonnier sat in his chair behind the counter, reading a book. Nothing had changed. Stuff was still stacked to the ceiling; stuff still hung down to the floor. R. Sonnier looked up. His eyes were flat, incurious.

"Can I help you?"

"It's me, Mr. Sonnier. Opal Foote. I've come to get my baroque marble that you've been saving for me."

"What marble? I don't have any marbles."

Patiently Sister Opal explained about the baroque pearl she had asked him to save for her last fall, and then she expectantly waited for the shock of recognition, the rummaging in a desk drawer, and the uncovering of the baroque pearl. She hadn't even yet seen it up close or held it. R. Sonnier looked annoyed.

"Listen, young lady, I had a baroque pearl last fall, and I sold it to a very nice lady who comes in here often to buy things. I never save anything except for my good customers. This lady paid me by check right away. I don't run any lay-away plan here, and that baroque pearl was priced at almost five hundred collars."

"You sold it? But it was supposed to be *mine!* I worked after school all fall and winter long, and I earned the money for it!" Sister Opal pulled out her wad of money. R. Sonnier looked astounded.

"Little lady, how was I to know you were serious? We get people in here every day saying they like something and they'll be back the next day or next week. They never show up, never! So when somebody comes in and says I'll take that ring or that vase, here, here's the money, why I *sell* it to them. I'd go out of business if I believed everything people tell me. But since you've worked all that time, maybe you'd like to see some nice earrings I've got, jade and . . ."

"No. I was starting a famous marble collection. I don't want anything else." Sister Opal tucked her worthless money away in her old purse and went out with her back straight and stiff.

She walked around downtown all day long, looking into bookstores, department stores, stationery shops, jewelry stores, boutiques, but nothing seemed attractive to her. She thought it was strange that all the times she hadn't had any money hundreds and hundreds of things in the store windows had looked so great and she had really wanted them. Now that she had a lot of money nothing interested her. She stared at the most exotic clothes without even a twinge of desire. Her beautiful baroque pearl belonged to somebody else; she didn't want any other thing. She put off going home as long as possible, but when the lights began to come on she knew it was time to go back.

The family was at supper. Every head turned to Sister Opal as she came in and slumped into her chair.

"Well!" boomed Roy, who didn't work Saturday nights. "Let's see that solid gold marble you got!"

Sister Opal's mother, who saw something was wrong, said, "Well, what's the trouble, Sister? Was the store closed?" Sister Opal, who had not cried, or even felt much of anything except emptiness and loss, burst into a howl she didn't even know was inside her.

"He sold it to somebody else a long time ago-o-oo-o!" Between sobs, hiccups, and tears dripping into her plate, Sister Opal told the family about R. Sonnier and how he had sold the pearl. Andrew was indignant and declared that if he was ever in the market for a baroque pearl, he would rather die in the gutter than buy it from R. Sonnier.

But Sister Opal's father said judiciously, "Well, Sister, he didn't do it out of spite and meanness. He was just being businesslike. If you were a storeman and somebody breezed in and said, 'Here, you hold on to that stuffed elephant for me, I'll be back someday and pay for it,' and a week later somebody else came in and said, 'Here, here's a thousand dollars for that stuffed elephant,' you *know* you are going to sell that elephant right there and then. Sister Opal, you should have checked back with that R. Sonnier every week or so, so that he'd know you were really serious about buying it. I know you're disappointed. I'm disappointed myself. I was looking forward to seeing that baroque pearl and knowing somebody in our family owned it." This brought a fresh howl from Sister Opal which her father silenced by continuing.

"As I see it, Sister, you can either curl up and die because you didn't get your fancy marble, or you can hurry up and quit crying and think about the future. Probably you should take that pearl money and put it with the college money so that you can study up on baroque pearls when you get to college. So you got to adopt a long range plan now and think about education and a career. . . ."

Sister Opal heard her father talking on in a

kindly way about his favorite subjects — education and getting knowledge and getting ahead and having a career. She knew that most of what he was saying was sensible, but she had heard it all so many times she didn't want to hear it again. Her father didn't *know* how it felt to be a girl and to want a beautiful thing very badly. Sister Opal excused herself from the table and went to her room. She flung herself on the bed sideways and dangled her head off the edge, looking at the pale rectangle of the window. The marble jar was dark in the twilight and it glittered along one side from the reflected light of the street lamp. Sister Opal reached out for the marble jar, tipped the contents onto the bed with a rich, sensuous, rolling sound. Her thin hand slid through the marble pile in the darkening room until she touched the familiar lopsided marble. Warming it in the hollow of her hand, she could just make out its ephemeral glow, its waxy luster against the darkness of her hand and the darkness of the oncoming night. She rolled it slightly in her palm and said softly to the warmed, heavy marble, "Oh, what a beautiful baroque pearl."

THE STREET WHERE MY HEART LIVES

ELLEN SCHAFFER CONFORD

When circumstances change, Sandy makes a last minute substitute of a possible dreamboat for an impossible dream.

For at least the hundredth time since September, Jane and I casually strolled past Mr. Arnold's house.

"Is he there?" I hissed, keeping my eyes carefully averted.

"Listen, Sandy, this is ridiculous," Jane said. "I must have walked fifty miles this year going down this block. My shoes are all worn out because of you. I mean, friendship can go just so far."

"He's not out?"

"Oh, sure he is. He's out there lying on a blanket in the middle of the snow getting a gorgeous suntan. Wow, look at those muscles!"

"Nobody likes a smart aleck," I said morosely.

"Well, I admire your optimism," she replied, "but since he hasn't been outside any of the other three hundred and fifty-eight times we've walked past his house, I really don't understand why we keep doing this. Don't you see enough of him in English to tide you over till the next day?"

"What can he say to me in class?" I demanded, "with thirty other kids he's supposed to be teaching and no privacy?"

Jane snorted. "The same thing he'd say to you if he saw you walk past his house. 'Hello, Sandy.'"

I sighed deeply. I really couldn't blame Jane for not being more sympathetic. Until the Real Thing hits you, you can't possibly understand how it feels: how your heart plunges down to your stomach when he looks at you, the special way he says your name when he takes the roll, the little smile that he can't quite hide when he calls on you to answer a question, how a forty-one-minute class passes in the blink of an eye or the flutter of a heartbeat. How could Jane possibly understand how I felt?

"You want to stop for a Coke?" Jane asked.

"No," I sighed, "I don't feel like it."

"Oh, come on, Sandy," she said impatiently. "This is asinine. You've got a perfectly ordinary crush on a teacher. It happens to ninety-nine percent of all teenage girls in the world. You're no different from the rest of us. Don't you ever read your mother's adolescent psychology books?"

"This *is* different," I said angrily.

"Hah!" she pounced. "That's the classic manifestation of the adolescent girl's crush on the older man. They all think 'this is different.' That just proves how undifferent you are."

41

There was no point in arguing with Jane. We'd been over the same ground for weeks, and she was still incapable of grasping the simple truth of the matter, which was that all those psych books are written by middle-aged, bearded Viennese doctors, who know as much about Real Love as I know about nuclear physics.

We walked the rest of the way to my house in silence.

"You want to come in for awhile?" I asked half-heartedly.

"Your enthusiasm is matched only by the graciousness of your invitation," she replied. "No, thanks. I have homework to catch up on."

She trudged off down the street and I went inside.

"Did you have a nice walk?" my mother asked as I started up the stairs.

"It was okay."

"I don't suppose you're going up to clean your room?" she hinted hopefully.

"You don't suppose correctly," I agreed. "I'm going to do my homework."

"That's a relief," she said. "I wasn't prepared to have the world come to an end."

"Sarcasm," I complained, "I'm surrounded by sarcasm."

I closed the door to my room a little bit louder than necessary and flopped on the bed. It was time to do some really serious thinking about the situation between Mr. Arnold and me. The school year wasn't getting any younger, and I had made absolutely no progress at all in my campaign to see him privately, outside the hallowed halls of learning. It isn't, I told myself, as if he doesn't want to see me.

It's just that he isn't sure I feel the same way about him as he feels about me. And also, of course, his job — he has to be very discreet about these things after all. He's probably just waiting until I graduate to approach me. But that won't be till next year! How can a tempestuous woman like me suppress this passion for another year and a half? For that matter, how can *he* wait that long to bare his soul?

The phone rang.

"Hello?"

"Hello, gorgeous."

"You must have the wrong number," I said coldly.

"Hey, dope, it's me, Chip."

"Oh. Hi."

"Try to control yourself, passion's plaything. The fire in your voice is searing the telephone wires."

It must have been National Sarcasm Week or something. All of a sudden everybody was Don Rickles.

"Did you call for a specific purpose, or merely to insure that your A.T.&T. stock goes up?" Oh, great, now *I* was doing it!

"I see you've been reading your *How to Be Popular* book again. Listen, I called to tell you that I just found out from Mr. Yaeger (our history teacher) that Mr. Arnold's wife just had a baby."

"His wife!" I cried.

"Well, they say wives make better mothers than husbands do."

Chip jabbered on, something about us all contributing a dollar for a present, but I wasn't able to listen.

Mr. Arnold was *married*. Why hadn't I ever considered that possibility? Possibility? No, *probability*. Of course he'd be married. A handsome, educated, charming man like that was not likely to escape the clutches of some scheming female forever. But why, why, I moaned inwardly, couldn't he have waited for my clutches! Misery welled up in me, and I felt all my emotions tangle into one gigantic double knot.

But what was I to do? I mean, you can't turn love on and off like a water faucet. The fact that he was married (unhappily, no doubt) really didn't change anything. I still loved him. I still felt the same churning in my insides when I pictured his face in my mind. His wife (probably a shrew who nagged him unmercifully) couldn't change that.

I couldn't contain myself with the awful news any longer. I just had to tell someone how destroyed my life was – you can't carry a burden like that all by yourself.

When Chip hung up, I called Jane.

"Jane!" I moaned. "I just had the most horrible news."

"Good grief, you sound like the Voice of Doom. What is it?"

"It's Mr. Arnold — he's *married*. His wife just had a baby."

"So?"

"For Pete's sake, aren't you listening to me? He's *married!*"

"So he's married. What did you expect him to be, a monk?"

"You idiot, don't you see? This is the end of everything for us."

"Somehow," Jane said drily, "I don't think this

will change your relationship with Mr. Arnold one bit."

"You're a really terrific friend, you know that?" I said bitterly. "Really right there when I need you. Full of sympathy and understanding."

"Look," Jane said, "I'm sorry if it came as such a shock to you, but I really don't see that it makes any difference. He's just as likely to fall madly in love with you now as if he were single, right? So don't let his being married alter your attitude one bit. You go right on mooning over him like you have been; your chances of running off to Tahiti with him are just as good as ever."

"Thanks for nothing, bosom buddy," I snapped. "So long, homewrecker."

I don't think I slept that night at all. I just lay awake, staring at the lines the light made through the venetian blinds, aching with the dull certainty of hopelessness. I got up a few times to confide some added misery to my diary or to jot down a couple of despair-filled lines of poetry, but mostly I just lay there under my patchwork quilt of tattered dreams.

Of all the little ironies life had in store for me, surely the harshest was doled out the next day. The class decided just before Mr. Arnold came in to have Chip and me pick out the present we were all buying for Mr. Arnold's new baby. Talk about the fickle finger of fate. This was as fickle a finger as had ever pointed out a victim for slow torture.

"We ought to be able to get something nice for thirty dollars," Chip speculated as we walked into Mayer's Department Store.

.We took the escalator up to Juvenile Furniture, and Chip wandered around aimlessly for awhile, checking price tags and looking bewildered.

Finally a salesman spotted us and came to the rescue.

When Chip told him what we had to spend and why, he said, "Here's just the thing." He led us over to a row of baby strollers and began extolling the virtues of one particular model that had collapsible sides, a sunshade, a basket for packages, and an assortment of straps that looked like the kid would be in a straitjacket every time you buckled him in.

The picture formed in my mind, ugly and unbidden. Mr. Arnold and his wife (short and fat), strolling down the block pushing junior along in his Tote-a-Tot, walking right past me as I slunk, wretched and forgotten, in the opposite direction. His wife (four feet eight, two hundred and thirty pounds), gabbling about how a baby cemented a marriage, and how glad she was that *he* wanted fourteen children too, never even noticing the pathetic victim of unrequited love that whimpered gently as they walked by.

"What do you think, Sandy?" Chip was asking.

"You'd be happier not knowing," I said gloomily.

"I mean about the stroller."

"Super. Buy it."

"Somehow you don't sound sincere," he observed. "Do you really think it's a good idea? I mean, maybe they have one already. It seems like everybody gets a stroller when they have a kid."

"Well, if they have one already they can always use this one for a planter."

"The young lady would like to see something else?" the salesman asked haughtily.

"You'll have to excuse her," Chip whispered to him. "She hasn't been the same since Valentino died."

The salesman was backing away from us warily when Chip said, "Okay, we'll take it."

"Boy, you sure acted weird," said Chip as we struggled to get the bulky carton out of the store. "What's the matter with you lately?"

"My soul is weary," I said bleakly. "My candle is ready to burn at both ends, and I haven't even got a match."

"Thanks for the explanation," he said. "Remind me not to ask again."

We managed to get the blasted thing on a bus and rode out to the stop a block away from Mr. Arnold's house. The bus driver, turning surly as we wrestled the carton out the narrow back exit of his vehicle, slammed the door practically on my skirt and sped away, as if fearful we might change our minds and climb back on again.

Half dragging, half carrying my end of the box toward No. 27, I began to absentmindedly hum "On the Street Where You Live" in a plaintive minor key, but Chip looked at me strangely so I stopped. Nobody loves you when you're down and out.

As we staggered up the walk, my heart began to pound. No matter how depressing the circumstances, I was at last going to see Mr. Arnold as a civilian. This was his house, that was his car, this was the driveway he must have shoveled, that, the door his key turned in every afternoon. I dropped my end of the box on the stoop.

"Urrggh," Chip grunted, under the sudden extra weight. "You might have warned me."

"Sorry about that," I said.

Chip rang the bell.

I stood paralyzed as the door finally opened.

He was wearing the most beautiful dirty sweatshirt in the world. He was barefoot. He was splattered with lemon yellow paint.

"Well, hi, this is a surprise," he smiled. "I was just painting the baby's room. I'm a new father."

I hate you, Mrs. Arnold, I seethed. I hate all two hundred and thirty pounds of you. Haven't you heard about the population explosion, you irresponsible woman?

"We heard," Chip said, "so we got a real surprise for you. Sandy and I, on behalf of your entire English IIIB class, wish to present you with this small token — unmpf," he groaned, trying to heave the carton up to present it to Mr. Arnold, "of our good wishes to you and your wife."

I abstain, I thought bitterly. I am not part of this tragic farce. I am merely window dressing, like the losing candidate asking us all to unite behind the winning candidate, and then going home to kick the dog and sulk.

"Thank you," Mr. Arnold beamed. "That's really great. My wife will be so pleased." From the lettering on the box, he had deduced it held a stroller.

"I hope you haven't got one already," Chip said. "We weren't sure."

"No, no, we haven't; we were planning to get one — oh, this is really something. You kids are too much."

He sounded sincerely delighted. I myself could

not have gotten that worked up over a stroller, but I myself have never been a new father. This display of paternal emotionalism was getting to me.

He asked us in, and he and Chip hauled the carton into the middle of the living room. Mr. Arnold went to get something to pry the box open.

On the piano there was a framed photograph of a woman. Good grief, I thought, what an egomaniac she must be. Imagine putting a picture of yourself right in the middle of your living room. The woman is a narcissistic exhibitionist.

Casually I walked over to examine the photograph. My fading hopes grew dimmer still. The woman in the picture was not quite two hundred and thirty pounds. My estimate had been approximately one hundred and twenty pounds off. Her hair was long and blonde, her eyes big and dark, with the most obviously false eyelashes since Twiggy. She was, in short, as ugly as Elizabeth Taylor.

"Here we go," said Mr. Arnold, slitting open the carton with a knife. "Hey," he said, pulling the cardboard apart, "it's collapsible. Hey, this is beautiful."

"What's going on?"

I looked up from the picture and stared into the most beautiful brown eyes I'd ever seen. My heart did the down-to-the-stomach bit, and proceeded to pound so hard it could have been heard next door.

The beautiful brown eyes stared back at me, and I heard, distinctly, Mr. Arnold introducing his kid brother Ken, who was a freshman at MIT, home on vacation.

Ken was definitely not paternal looking. He admired the stroller politely, but not effusively. He seemed to take as little interest in the mechanics of collapsible carriages as any normal, sensible, gorgeous person.

"That was a nice thing for you all to do," he said, looking specifically at me. He didn't say "you kids" I noted approvingly.

I smiled, trying to keep my whole heart from pouring out along with the smile.

"MIT," I marveled, "you must really have worked to get into such a good school.

For a full ten seconds I pondered my amazing comeback from the depths of stark tragedy, my incredible good fortune at discovering a new, improved Mr. Arnold, the last-minute substitution of a possible dreamboat for an impossible dream — for ten seconds I pondered the strange surprises life has in store for us.

Then I looked warmly at Ken Arnold and began to calculate the distance to MIT.

THE COVER-UP

JOAN DASH

The club is for the Beautiful People . . . not for a girl like Marcia.

Each weekday morning since the warm weather began, Marcia and Joe had been taking a bus out to the Overlake Country Club to spend the morning at the pool. Marcia would sit in a deck chair with a terry robe over her suit, baby oil on her face, and *War and Peace* in her lap; Joe couldn't wait to get in the water. He was always after her to swim with him; he'd beg, wheedle, even threaten to throw her into the pool, but she'd just smile and point to the book and tell him to get cracking on his backstroke or his butterfly. Joe had signed up for the first three weeks of August at a camp for retarded children, and he wanted to get into their advanced swimmer group. It was Joe's special goal for the summer, that advanced swimmer group; so it was also Marcia's goal for him, 'and each time she turned a page, she'd look up to

51

check on his progress, wave and nod encouragement.

He was terrific in the water. Since Joe's arms and legs were mildly palsied, the regular exercise of swimming was just what he needed; something he needed even more was a way of competing with his brother and sister. At swimming Joe did more than compete; he outclassed his sister Marcia and their brother Nat. When an aunt of theirs had joined Overlake Club and talked the management into letting Joe and Marcia use the pool, Joe's whole outlook changed. His summer stopped being a yawning gap between the end of school and the start of August and became instead a triumphant succession of mornings in the water. Marcia had originally planned on being a junior counselor at Girl Scout camp that summer — she was fifteen and eligible — but she gave up her plans like a shot, for Joe's sake.

"Hey, Marsh," he called to her, a whining edge to his voice, "put down your book and have me a race. I bet I beat the stuffings out of you, backstroke."

She shook her head briskly, "Now don't start that, Joe. Let's see some racing turns."

He was hanging off the pool's edge and looking up at her; his eyes were bright with excitement, peering past the streams of water from his dark hair. When she saw him like that, with just his head sticking out of the water, Marcia couldn't help thinking he looked like any fourteen-year-old. A person couldn't tell, seeing only the shining, water-slick head, that he was really more like seven or eight.

"Aw, come on," Joey begged. "What's the use of being here if you never swim once?"

She shook her head quickly. "I have to get through my book." He sighed a little, then shoved off and backstroked, conscious of her watching him. She returned to the book, but Joey's sigh weighed on her, saddened her; she knew that if Nat were here, he'd be right in the water with Joe. He'd be racing him, having water fights with him; he'd be standing in the pool with his legs apart, and Joe would be swimming through them, like an eel.

Only I'm not Nat, Marcia thought. And Nat had found a job, the first week of summer, selling books in a downtown store. He was the only seventeen-year-old in the place; all the other temporaries were college kids. Of course it was hard on the rest of them, on Mom and Dad as well as on Marcia, because Nat was Joe's hero. His absence had left Joe at loose ends at first; last summer they had played ball for hours, just the two of them sometimes, and sometimes with half the neighborhood kids joining in. Well, Marcia thought, you can't have everything. She couldn't play ball with Joe, she didn't feel at all like swimming with him, but she was doing her bit all the same, doing more than Nat, actually, getting Joe down here every day, spurring him on, applauding him.

All the same, once she'd thought about Nat, his absence semed to haunt her; it slowed down her reading, and she had to go back over each paragraph, aware that she hadn't quite caught its meaning. She put her book down at last and leaned back in the chair with her eyes closed. She recalled a morning two weeks ago when Joe had stomped into Marcia's room and said, "How come Nat's getting dressed so early?"

"He's going to his job in the bookstore," Marcia told him.

"Again? He went there last week."

Marcia had smiled. "It's a regular job, just the way Dad has a regular job. It's every day all summer long."

Nat, shaved and dressed now, came out of the bathroom and stood in the doorway while he tied his tie. "Nine to five, with a measly half-hour for lunch," he told his brother.

"It really is like Pop," Joe said. He looked up sharply at Nat and said, his eyes blinking rapidly, "I'm awfully proud of you, Nat!"

Marcia remembered how tears had jumped to her eyes at those words, how she had ducked her head so Joe wouldn't see. When she looked up, Nat had walked across the room and thrown his arms around Joe in a bear hug. "I'm proud of you too, Big Joe," Nat told him.

She thought, well, so am I. So am I proud of Joe. Only some people could say certain things easily, naturally, while other people couldn't. Just as some people could do certain things, like Nat, who'd be in the water with Joe right this minute. . . .

It's the shyness, she thought. If I weren't so shy I wouldn't be sitting here with a terry cover-up over a one-piece swimsuit. The Overlake Club was no place for a shy girl, a stranger, an intruder. Everything about the place breathed Money. Everyone in it was loaded and dressed to show it.

The kids her age poured out of fancy sports cars, and their manners, their words, their very accents hinted at influence and private schools.

She stiffened a bit in her chair. Joe was talking to someone. Although he was the friendliest kid in the world, even Joey had caught on that people around here were different, not at all like the people in Laurelwood, where he'd lived all his life. So he curbed his friendliness somewhat. But he had bumped, quite literally, into someone in the pool, a grown woman. Marcia could see only her head in its sequined cap. Perhaps the bumping had made Joe forget where he was, for he was talking away as if he were home.

"I'm sorry I rammed you. I'm practicing up for camp in August. Want to have me a race, backstroke?" They were only a couple of yards from Marcia. She couldn't hear all Joe's words, not exactly, but she could tell from his lips what he was saying.

The woman was treading water and smiling politely. She must surely be wondering why a four-teen-year-old was rattling on like that.

"I can even beat my big brother, backstroke," he said. "I have a brother, Nat, and a sister, Marcia. How many kids in your family?"

Marcia saw the woman's smile quiver a bit — she'd caught on by now — and then the woman went one way and Joey, with a puzzled shrug, swam off the other way.

I wish we had a pool like this in Laurelwood, Marcia thought. In Laurelwood she'd be in the water all day long. She wouldn't have to wear a dumb one-piece, tank-type suit, either. She'd have a cute two-piece; she was certainly old enough. But here — well, between knowing she didn't belong and being a bit shy about her figure to start with, it seemed easier to sit by the pool in a safe one-piece suit with a terry cover-up for good measure.

If the pool had been in Laurelwood, they could even let Joe come by himself any time he wanted. But here you didn't dare take a chance; who knew what might be said or done, or even if something might happen to bring on one of Joe's rare temper tantrums. Then there'd be all these strangers staring at Joe out of their hard eyes.

For there was something hard, or perhaps brittle, about these people. From time to time one of the kids had stopped at Marcia's chair and tried a few polite words. But there was always something stiff and distant about them; it didn't take much, in the way of pointing at her book, to get them to march off and go on about their business. She could tell they didn't really want her, that only curiosity made them stop at her chair, wondering where she'd picked up that crummy terry robe. They, the girls who belonged to this place, had cover-ups to match their suits.

At that very moment a girl in a white bikini was poised on the high-dive board. Her suit looked like white piqué, her suntan was perfect, a thick gold bangle glittered on one upraised arm. Joe, at the pool's edge, near Marcia, was staring up at the girl, who rose briskly into the air and sailed toward the water in an elegant swan dive.

Joey blinked and turned to Marcia. "You could do that. Easy as pie. You could do a better swan than that girl, couldn't you, Marsh?"

She laughed. "Don't be silly, Joe. You know I'm scared to death of diving."

"Well," he said, "then if you would quit being scared, you could do it. Just quit being scared." He stuck his head under water and tried reaching for his toes, stiff-legged.

If I quit being scared, Marcia thought, I could even get away with a white bikini. She realized that even at home she'd feel odd, parading around in a pair of handkerchiefs. There was something embarrassing about summer and swimsuits, something altogether exposed and naked, knowing everyone was looking at you, measuring you. Quit being scared? She thought, we're not all like you, Joey. We can't all be as brave as you.

She returned to the book. Halfway down the page, she realized that someone was walking toward her, two people actually, and one was the white bikine girl. The other was, of all people, Bruce Stadler. He'd been in her art class last year at Laurelwood. He was an attractive boy and popular.

"Marcia! Can you beat that?" He ran up to her, the girl lagging behind him. "Marcia, meet my friend Tracy. Marcia and I used to paint together, Tracy."

Marcia half rose, nodding at Tracy. "That was a neat dive," she said.

Tracy smiled. She was a neat-looking girl altogether, slim and muscular, with the kind of walk people achieve when they know they're good at every sport they try. "Golly, but it wore me out, all that showing off," Tracy said.

Bruce and Tracy pulled up a chaise and sprawled out on it, Tracy in the seat part and Bruce balanced over the end. There was something about the way they did this, something friendly and casual and easy, that made Marcia realize they weren't just pals or acquaintances, but steadies. They looked so used to each other, Marcia thought. Tracy has it made.

"We moved here around the middle of June," Bruce said. "My dad says there's no telling how long we can afford to keep it up, but until the bank takes back the house, I plan on sopping up every expensive minute at this club." Then he leaned back, his spine supported by Tracy's legs.

Marcia smiled, thinking it was rather lovely of him to be so frank. Instead of casting about for some way to get rid of the two, she said, "We're still living in Laurelwood; we're just using my aunt's membership here."

"Great," Bruce said. "You should show up more often, catch some of the dances."

Marcia shivered. The thought of dances here was a shivery one, but she certainly didn't want them to know it, especially not Tracy. Tracy had her head flung back, her eyes closed, and the straps of her skimpy top down, to soak up the sun. Sleepily and in an offhand way, she said, "I'm chairman of something or other connected with the dances. Hospitality, I think. So consider this a hospitable invitation, Marcia. We're having a square dance Wednesday night. Y'all come."

Marcia nodded. She decided Tracy bugged her the least bit — so tan, so competent, so "in" she was dispensing hospitality like a princess. She said nothing, just nodded. Tracy shifted and opened her eyes.

"You will come, won't you?" she demanded.

"We could really use some new blood around this place; everything's gotten so cliquey and inbred. Know what I mean?"

Marcia waved, in a vague and general way; let her take it however she wanted to. Tracy's eyes wandered. Bruce was riffling through *War and Peace*, reading Marcia's penciled comments in the margins.

"I guess it's because I've lived here forever and ever," Tracy said. Then she stopped. She had seen someone in the water; her eyes were following that someone slowly across the pool. She ran one hand through her streaky blonde hair; sunlight bounced off the heavy gold bracelet. It was an old-fashioned, thick bangle with scrollwork.

Good grief, Marcia thought. Imagine wearing a thing like that in the water. It was typical of girls like Tracy, girls who were born into country clubs. They owned red-gold heirloom bracelets, but instead of keeping them socked away in tissue paper, they wore them swimming, in chlorinated pools.

Then Tracy broke into pealing laughter, her head thrown back. She tapped Bruce on the shoulder. "Will you just look at that, Brucie. Talk about uncoordinated!"

"Leave me alone. I'm busy with Tolstoi."

"No, look out there, will you?" Tracy had popped out her eyes and opened her mouth in grotesque imitation. Lightly pointing with one slim finger, the bangle shooting golden rays, she tried to get him to look up, and Marcia's eyes followed the finger. Joe. Joey in the water, trailing a pair of teenagers, a boy and a girl swimming tandem with their arms lined.

He looked more like a seal than a boy, now; he

looked like a friendly pup of a seal, and his arms were flippers. He wasn't simply swimming, Joey was reaching out to those two, begging for their attention. His mouth was wide open, his eyes round and large, his movements jerky and fitful.

"Did you ever see anything like it? He's paddling after Petey and Evelyn, the lovebirds," Tracy said. "It's the funniest thing I ever saw in my life."

"He isn't paddling," Marcia snapped. "How can you say he's paddling? He's doing a lovely side-stroke. He does a darn good butterfly, and the finest backstroke you ever saw. How can you laugh, how dare you —" but her voice began to shake. She had plenty more to say to this monster, to this she-devil in a white bikini, but she had to wait for her voice to calm down.

Meanwhile Joe looked up. He'd become aware of Tracy's face, and of her interest. And of Bruce, looking up too, shooting a hand out and laying a finger across Tracy's mouth. Bruce knew about Joe.

Marcia's eyes were wet. If I cry in front of her, I'll kill her, she thought. She saw Joey swim toward them. Then he climbed out, neatly and nicely, and walked over the tiles by the edge of the pool. But when he walked, his legs were floppy and his feet turned out the way they sometimes did. His arms looked loose and jangly. No, Joey, no, Marcia thought. Mind your arms, point your feet forward, she's watching every move you make.

"That was a fine sidestroke, Joey," Marcia told him, when he stopped in front of them.

Joey nodded, spraying her and Bruce with drops of water. His eyes were on Tracy. "I saw you swan dive. Boy, you were great. I told my big sister Marcia . . ."

Marcia interrupted him. Ignoring Tracy, she said to Bruce, "This is my brother, Joe. Joe, this is Bruce. He used to go to Laurelwood. That's his friend, Tracy," still not looking at the girl.

Joey nodded again, only harder, so he sprayed all over *War and Peace,* and a fine crystal wash blew backward into Tracy's face.

Tracy swiped at it, quickly, then stuck out a hand. "How do you do, Joe," she said. It was hard for Marcia to tell what the tone of her voice suggested: irony, faint amusement, mockery? Or was she going to be kind, a princess condescending to a freak? I'll choke her if she's kind, Marcia thought; I'll throttle her if she dares to condescend.

"I told Marsh she could dive like you any old day if she'd quit being scared," Joe told Tracy.

They were shaking hands, and that cryptic look was still on Tracy's face. A dull flush glowed under her suntan. Marcia was listening and watching her so hard that her muscles ached with tension.

"Listen, Tracy," Joe said. "Come on into the water, and I'll do my backstroke for you. After that you could show me racing dives. I'm not allowed on the high board, but I do racing dives off the edge. You could show me. Please? I need someone to swim with, you know."

Marcia gripped the arms of her chair, her eyes glued to Tracy's hard eyes, her sealed, unmoving lips.

But Tracy said nothing. She jumped to her feet in one neat movement, she tugged at the bot-

61

tom of her suit, pushed up the gold bangle and walked to the pool's edge. She dove in expertly, then flicked back her short hair and called up to Joe, "Hurry up, then, let's see your backstroke."

His whole face lit up. He slid into the pool and pulled ahead of her with his beautiful, gliding stroke, water spurting from his mouth like a whale. The pair of them moved in rhythm to the middle of the pool where Joey spotted a yellow ball. He flipped over and skidded it to Tracy, and she skidded it back, and on they went, sidestroke now, the yellow ball scudding between them. Marcia could no longer see Joey's face. She didn't want to see it.

Her body had sagged, her muscles had gone lax and there was a sick feeling in her stomach. She became aware of a figure standing behind Bruce. A chunky blond boy was watching the pair in the water. Bruce, leaning forward, whispered to Marcia, "Don't mind Tracy — what she said before. She's a good kid underneath, she really is."

Marcia nodded. She wasn't actually listening to Bruce. She couldn't hear what he said to the boy behind him after that, although she knew they were watching her. She knew they could tell, when she stood up, that tears were sliding down her face. She walked to the edge of the pool and ripped off her terry robe and let it drop.

In that sudden moment of near-nakedness, her robe and her shyness no longer protecting, excusing, enclosing her, Marcia felt a puff of cool air about her shoulders. Her bones felt somehow locked in place. What now, she wondered. Should she do a bad dive, with those boys behind her, their eyes glued to her skinny shoulder blades, or a sloppy slide-in? Or should she wait here until her bones unlocked, until she could make a decent try at a dive? Should she stand here forever, while all those beautiful, well-dressed strangers came and went around the pool and both boys waited with folded arms and made bets on how long she'd stay rooted to that spot? She wished she had the robe back on, she wished she were back in her chair with her shyness in place, she wished she never had Joe for a brother.

Joe and Tracy were chasing each other. They were a pair of dolphins playing water games; they were fish, they were tadpoles. Sprays of water flew about them, shooting rainbows.

Marcia shut her eyes, thinking, you can't change the past. It's only the future you can change. Then she threw herself at the water. "Wait for me, you guys," she yelled, hearing how shrill, how frantic her voice was.

She saw Tracy smile and turn toward her; that smile was warm and simple and direct. It was also — Marcia tried not to hold it against her — a well-bred smile, a lady's smile.

I'm trying, Marcia told herself; I may not succeed but I'll try to forgive that girl for everything: for the dive, for the bracelet, for Bruce, for the Junior League smile, and for knowing more about Joe than his own sister did.

Joe? He was smiling too. The seal-pup look was gone from his face; he looked alert and sharp now. "Hey, Marsh," he said, "you're a *good* swimmer once you get going."

She swallowed a mouthful of warm, chlorinated

water and felt again that knot way back in her throat, like a clump of tears. And from the corner of her eyes she saw two little kids running round the pool on sneakered feet, right over the terry robe, leaving sopping footprints. Who needs it, she thought. Who needs that thing to hide behind?

"So are you, Big Joe," she told him. "So are you."

NEW GIRL

ELIZABETH ALLEN

Mary Jo is confused. So many people are trying to get into the Right Crowd. What is the Right Crowd *and why is it so important?*

MONDAY

Well, dear Diary, here I am, a new girl in a new school. You may be seeing quite a lot of me until I get settled and acquainted and all. Dad says we'll be here for my sophomore to senior year and that's a promise. It's such a relief to be settled! We've lived in so many different places. . . .

I hardly remember Caracas, except that I was scared when I couldn't understand what people were saying (but before I knew it I was talking Spanish!), and Canada is a dim memory too, except that it could be so terribly cold. Anyway, I'm glad I'm here in this southwestern city. The last place we lived in was such a small town. And I'm thrilled with our house and yard and the "playroom." (It's remodeled from a garage, but just great.) I'm especially thrilled about Hoover High. Hoover's had more Merit Scholarship Finalists than any school in the state. It's supposed to be a wonderful place.

I'm a little scared of a new school; you always are at first. And it's bad transferring in the middle of the year like this. But I expect to get along all right. I always have. Of course, I've grown another four stringbean inches, and there's simply too much yardage in Mary Jo. . . . Dear Diary, you may be seeing a lot of me.

TUESDAY

Well, here I am, bleeding. Hoover High is roughly the size of the Los Angeles airport, and not only does it have the highest scholastic rating in the Southwest; I've also heard that it has the highest suicide rate. (Can that be true?) All I could think of when I walked in was that I was too tall, my hair was too long and too straight and just plain old brown — I was nothing. I've never felt that way before!

There is some rule here that no matter what direction you are going in the hall, somebody else is going the other direction. There are forty people in my English class, and I got lost trying to find the gym, and got lost again trying to find the office. When I asked one boy where the cafeteria was, he said he had no idea, he never ate there!

My lockermate is a scared-looking little blonde girl who is also new. She says the secret of getting along at Hoover is to find the right crowd. I asked her how you found the Right Crowd, but she doesn't know. My adviser is a kindly soul who says, "You will love the friendly atmosphere of Hoover." There was a special talent assembly today, and a girl played the piano — I thought she was a visiting concert artist, but she's a junior at Hoover! What a place!

At three thirty I left, and who should I find myself walking along with but Jan (the scared-looking blonde), so I thought that naturally we'd walk on together. But she said, "Bye," and disappeared into the crowd. The right one, I trust.

WEDNESDAY

Poor Mom is exhausted. I got home from school today (still bleeding) and I wanted to tell her about things, but she'd been fixing curtains, and waiting for the telephone man to come, and unpacking — and then there are the boys. I thought with Bunny in nursery school and Jake in first grade they'd calm down, but I guess not. She'd had to go to Jake's school (he'd eaten an eraser) and she was also having second thoughts about the house. My folks bought it because of the location and the big yard and playroom, and now she thinks the bedrooms are too small.

Of course, I've been having "second thoughts" too. I'd been homesick for all the other places we've lived. I've been homesick for Canada! The winters are cold, all right, but I finally learned how to bundle up and keep warm. Of course, I didn't mention any of this to Mom.

I know Mom has a lot to do, but I wonder when she'll get around to me? It's bad enough to have plain old brown hair and plain old brown eyes;

but besides that, I'm too tall, and my skin's not the best, and my clothes are a sight. I've let down my skirts and pressed them, but they look queer. I've always done my own laundry because Mom has enough to do with the boys and all, but my stuff just doesn't look right.

And I'm still bleeding.

Jan still hasn't found out about the Right Crowd, and if she did I doubt if she'd tell me.

FRIDAY
The girls at Hoover have such pretty clothes. I know now that they aren't all rich; they don't all have fathers who own oil companies; but the fact is that they *look* rich. These girls wear matching sweater and skirt sets, and tailored jackets, and cute frilly blouses, and all kinds of shoes.

I keep telling myself *Clothes aren't that important.* But you have to look like the other kids. You have to have what the other kids have — if you don't, you're dead.

SATURDAY
My first week at Hoover is finished, and I am still bleeding. Things have got to get better. They can't get worse.

MONDAY
Jan and I have the same lunch hour and we usually sit together; she isn't exactly good company, because she just sits and talks about the "popular" kids, but it's better than nothing. Today, though, I couldn't find Jan. Sometimes that girl just disappears. I got my tray in the cafeteria, and sat at a

table. A bunch of kids who are in first hour with me were there, but they had to get up and go to Spanish. They said, "See you," and left. Some other kids came. Then they saw someone they knew and went across the room to another table. Next to me were a bunch of girls who are all in the same Social Club. They sat there talking. "Yes, she's pinned," one of them said. "Yes, I do like him, but he won't ask for a date because of my steady." "No, she's not pinned." The girls spoke only to each other. They talked as though there were no one else in that big room.

No one else was.

I am not going to let all this get me down. I *refuse*.

My brothers have built a marvelous fort! They found an old slide nobody wanted and pushed it up to a crate, and I helped them slide down into their own little secret place where no one can find them.

I was tempted to try it myself (I'm thin enough to make it) but, after all, I'm *sixteen*.

What can I do?

Where can I go?

TUESDAY

A girl in my English class looked sort of familiar to me today, and sure enough I had known her in Casper. Her name is Myra and she's nice, although she's gotten so fat I hardly recognized her. I thought I'd finally found somebody else to eat lunch with, but she goes home for lunch every day; she's on a diet. Myra is worried about the Right

Crowd too. I've never coped with this Right Crowd stuff before.

Poor old Jan, who has these big blue eyes and would be pretty if she'd relax, is still trying to find out about Crowds. If you get in the Wrong Crowd, she says, it's fatal. Every day we start out of Hoover High together, and every day she says, "Bye!" and goes off alone. I go off alone.

It's silly. It's more than silly; it's stupid.

I'm beginning to wonder if I will ever make it. Maybe this time I won't learn the language. Maybe this time I'll never get warm.

WEDNESDAY

You'd think that with no social life I'd have plenty of time to study and would at least do well with my grades, but it isn't working out that way at all. I got a "progress slip" in English today, which means I am not making progress. I've got to stop feeling sorry for myself and just *work*. A tiny little girl named Dot, who is in gym with me, said that she understood my problem; she got all D's until she went out for activities, and joined a health club, and started dating, and now she gets all A's. She says it doesn't make sense (it doesn't).

Jake fell off the roof today while drinking a bottle of Coke, and the folks rushed him to the hospital. I wanted to go along, because I've always been sort of interested in hospitals, but I had to stay with Bunny.

I always have to stay with someone or something.

There wasn't a thing wrong with Jake; he was not even bruised! He's tough. *He'll* do all right at Hoover.

70

My dad tonight — I guess he thought he hadn't been paying too much attention to me — said, without thinking how it would sound, "Well, Mary Jo — Sweet Sixteen!"

THURSDAY
Sweet! Being sixteen is sour, bitter, cold.

Today, mother dragged me to a dermatologist, who took one look at me and gave me a list of things to Avoid Completely, such as fried food, ice cream, cheese, peanut butter, and chocolate. I have no idea how he knew all my favorites.

What's the matter with me? I should be glad to go to a dermatologist.

I'll study too.

Dear Diary, you will still see a lot of me, but not another line until things improve.

MONDAY
I cannot believe that my face is better after a few days of eating broiled meat and grass and slapping junk on at night, but it is. *And* my Spanish teacher found out I could speak well, although I'm weak in grammar, and now she talks back and forth to me all the time and we make jokes and all! Kind of fun. A boy named Sherwood called me. I have no idea who he is. Mom has gotten me a gold-colored jumper, "to bring out those brown eyes," and cotton material to make me dresses for spring. She pointed out that one advantage of being tall is that I can wear these new prints.

TUESDAY
Jan has told me to have nothing to do with Sher-

71

wood. (He turns out to be a boy in my Spanish class.) Sherwood rides a bike to school — at Hoover, where so many boys have cars — and carries his lunch to school in a paper sack. He will never, never be in the Right Crowd.

I mentioned this crowd bit to Mother, and she just sort of gasped.

"Mary Jo, did it ever occur to you to make your own crowd? There must be activities — you've got to jump into things! And we ought to give you a party in the playroom. . . ."

I started to tell her that I would have no one to ask to a party, but right then Bunny came in saying that Jake had hit him and then slid down into their fort and wouldn't let him come in, and by the time we got that straightened out Mom and I had sort of lost the thread of our conversation.

It was just as well. I really don't have anyone to invite to a party, and besides, our "playroom" isn't a clubroom, really; it's kind of makeshift, and there are cracks in the walls.

TUESDAY

We got our cards and I didn't do too badly. The only A was in Spanish, but the rest were B's and C's. Myra was undone because she got a D, but she's been so worried about her nonexistent social life and her weight. . . . Jan got all C's. Hoover has kids who get nothing but A's; always have. . . . Sherwood got A's except for typing and gym. He carries his lunch because he has to eat two; he's worried about his weight because he's thin.

I can't for the life of me see anything wrong about carrying your lunch in a sack.

I hope I can find someone to play tennis with soon. I'm not the champ I used to be, because ever since shooting up so fast, I've been uncoordinated, but I still love the game. There are good courts behind Hoover.

I hope I can get into volunteer work at one of the hospitals here this summer. I've always had a dream of going into some kind of hospital work.

But right now . . . yes, now. What? I'm not bleeding quite as much, but my social life's almost as nonexistent as Myra's.

Dear Diary, are you as sick of me as I am?

WEDNESDAY

I did something so dumb. Sherwood asked me for a date, and I turned him down. I know, I absolutely know, that I let Jan influence me. Oh, well.

Then I tried out for Swimettes, but didn't make it. I'm still on broiled meat and grass and it has helped my skin, but I've lost weight. . . . If I'd been able to go one more length, I'd have made it. Then I thought I'd try out for one of the choral groups. But at the last minute I hung back. Jan says only the Social Club kids make those groups.

Now I'm mad, mad at Jan and mad at everybody, but mostly just mad at myself. And I know that I hurt Sherwood's feelings. After all, boys have feelings too.

THURSDAY

Mom has really started pouncing on me! She is simply set on me having a teen party (the mere thought makes my blood run cold), and she's after me to do this and do that and to jump into things more. I am simply not the jumping type. I'll never be like Myra, afraid to try, or like poor little Jan, worrying away, but, as Mary Jo, I try some and that's that — I don't leap.

Hoover High is for leapers.

FRIDAY

I know now why that boy said to me that he never ate in the cafeteria. Some of the kids never do. They dash out in a car to a drive-in.

There are kids at Hoover who drive better cars than my dad's.

It's a strange school. There are bad things about it, but there are wonderful thing too. I am finally "in" something; there's a Spanish Club — you conduct all business in Spanish. If you are good at anything, have any skill or talent or aptitude, they try to make a spot for you at Hoover. Dot's in this club too, so I know someone in it.

And there's a Japanese student here (I haven't met him) and he sounds rough-and-tumble — he's on the wrestling team — but he wrote the most beautiful essay for *All School News* called, "My Two Countries."

In a way I hate Hoover, and yet I'm not sure I would change schools now, even if I could. I've been hurt here, and maybe I'll be hurt again, but maybe you have to get stomped on some to grow.

I wish I hadn't hurt Sherwood.

MONDAY

Today Mom grabbed me right after school and said she'd heard that a hospital here used high school girls as volunteers in the summer and that in order to do this you had to take their "Orientation" and go there this afternoon. She had the car, luckily, so off we went, in spite of the fact Jake's school had called because he'd put a rubber mouse in the teacher's desk. I was afraid that would wreck everything, but Mom simply said, "She should be glad it was not a real one," and off we went.

"I cannot give all my time to the boys," she muttered.

We had to take Bunny with us, but he behaves pretty well when he's not with Jake, and luckily he had his Trusty Interplanetary Disintegrating Flashlight Pistol to play with in the back seat.

Mom dropped me off at the hospital and told me what room to go to, and said she would be back in exactly an hour. She couldn't very well go with me because of Bunny and his Trusty Interplanetary etc., etc. I went to the room and at first my heart dropped, because there were a whole bunch of Social Club kids (they are always in everything) along with girls from other high schools. However, the girls from Hoover recognized me and called, "Come on over, Mary Jo!" and I joined them. Then Dot came in, and we called to her. A girl who is even taller than I am told me she had a uniform I could use, and gave me her candy-striped pinafore then and there. I never dreamed any "sosh" would be that nice!

What we do is take a short training course so that we won't goof off around the hospital, and then when school's out you go there three times a week and help with the mail cart or do errands, and all. We were shown around the hospital, and it's great. I'd be happy to scrub floors there.

Things are looking up. . . .

TUESDAY

Mom has finished two of my new dresses! One has huge pink flowers and one's a zebra print. . . . I love them!

I am about fed up with Jan. I told her about Spanish Club, and she said a school-sponsored club was nothing, and I mentioned candy-striping, and she said that it was a queer thing to do, and she keeps talking about Sherwood as though he were a J.D., or something. She's the one who is nothing.

SATURDAY

Yesterday Sherwood called. I was surprised, as he has been mad at me ever since I turned him down that time.

"C'mon," he said. "The Protest March for shorter class hours starts in ten minutes."

I said fine, I'd have my sign all ready, and he came by (not on his bike but in the family car!), and what we did was go to the movies. Afterward we came back here and played Ping-Pong in the playroom. Sherwood must be about seven feet tall.

I really feel a little less desperate. I have the candy-stripe thing to do this summer, and Dot and Myra for friends, and a boy interested in me — I bleed no more.

Jan just called. She wanted to know where I'd gotten my flowered cotton, and when I said Mom had made it she wouldn't believe me. Then she said I was lucky to have gotten in candy-striping, everyone's in it, and she tried to get in it too but it's too late. And then she told me that right now, just as everyone was beginning to notice me, to not make the mistake of being with absolutely the wrong people. She said that Myra and Dot are not the right people at all.

I almost said, "You are not the right person." I have got to pull away from Jan.

Sherwood called too. He wants to teach me to play chess; that should be interesting! He belongs to the Chess Club.

THURSDAY

Well! Just as I am beginning to feel quite cheerful about life, I run into Myra, and she is glooming all over the place. I have never quite seen such despair.

"Don't cut your throat all the way," I told her. "Leave the knife in; it'll draw more crowds."

"Very funny," she snarled. "Don't give me gas. I asked this boy from my Youth Group to come over and play Ping-Pong and stuff Friday night, and two other couples were coming too — really a sort of party, but relatives are coming, and I've got to call it off! Our clubroom is also our guest room."

I told her that this was a shame.

"Mom had said I could have a party because I've managed to lose fifteen pounds," she sighed. "Of course, Mom feels almost as bad about this as I do."

I went on to Spanish, and then a brilliant idea hit me. I found Myra at her locker and asked if she could have her party somewhere else. I was thinking, of course, of our playroom.

"Yes!" she said, and before we knew it we were making plans.

"Your 'coming out' party because you took some off," I told her, and she shrieked and fell into her locker, and we were both late for class.

As soon as I could I found Sherwood (he was out in back, making faces at the track team) and asked him if he could come to a party Friday night. He looked sort of surprised, and I told him it was just casual, he didn't need to dress up, but it turned out that he was simply surprised because I'd asked him to a party. He said he'd wear what he always wore to parties — shorts and a pith helmet!

When I saw Myra again, she asked me if I planned to include Jan. I wasn't sure.

"I've stop saying 'Hi' to her in the halls because she never answers back," Myra said. "But there will be an extra boy — maybe two — these boys just moved onto our street, and my folks know their folks and would like them included. So she could come."

"I'll think about it," I told her.

I did ask Dot, because I know she goes steady and that they're always looking for something to do.

I rushed home and told Mom. She was with the boys, making them clean up their room, which always looks like the city dump.

"A party?" she said, looking startled (she had a bird's nest in one hand and a pile of comic books in the other). "With one day's notice? I've been after you to have one, but I wanted to make you a dance dress and plan the color scheme — "

I tried not to shudder.

"It's to be casual," I told her, and I explained about Myra and how she had it all planned. "She's even got the soft drinks, and she'll bring her record player and records."

Mom agreed to it all, looking dazed, just as Bunny finally found all his dirty socks — he'd put them in a pillow cover and then zipped it up.

Jan called me. Her voice was all frosty and queer.

"What's this about you having a gig?" she asked.

"We just started putting it together," I told her. "And you're invited. There'll be a boy for you." I couldn't bear to leave her out.

"Well, if you're giving it with *Myra* . . . Mary Jo, she's not popular at all."

I made some excuse and hung up. I was not going to beg her to come; she's spoiled too many things for me, and she would, given half a chance, ruin this party.

Well . . . I wonder how it will be. . . .

SATURDAY

Wow! I don't know where to start!

When I heard them all coming, I died; I sank into my ankles; I wondered if I could faint or something and get out of it. . . . The playroom looked fine, with Mexican hats hung on the wall to hide the cracks, and Cokes and ginger ales cooling in a tub of ice. I didn't even have to worry about my brothers because Mom had taken them to a friend's. (She must be a pretty good friend.)

But I was scared. Talk about butterflies in the stomach! I felt as though there were bats in mine. Jan had called back and almost begged to come, and I'd said, "Fine," but the first time I heard her even mention the Right Crowd or the popular kids I would drop her down my brother's slide into the fort and she would never get out, never. Then I wondered about the new boys, and if Sherwood would really wear a pith helmet, and what Dot's steady would be like; and I was also realizing in absolute horror that none of these people knew each other and that in fact I didn't know all of them. What if they just all stood around and glared at each other?

Well, I needn't have worried. The neighbors called the police right after midnight (we hadn't realized that the amplifier on the new boy's guitar would blow everyone on the street out of bed!) and we promised to quiet right down, and unhooked the amplifier. Then, of course, we heard Jan, who was squawking away in the boy's fort, and had to let her out. This one boy kept getting up in a tree and making speeches (he was a mess), but the new boy's brother was nice, and a tennis champ, and offered to take me on. My folks kept coming out, asking us to calm down, but then they would sort of smile and leave. Myra looked perfectly beautiful and did this imitation of our English teacher, and Sherwood went around all evening in one of the Mexican hats, and he had found the Trusty Interplanetary Flashlight and insisted that he was disintegrating everybody. Dot, that little gentle thing, turned out to be taking karate! She can throw a man twice her weight across the room.

(She offered to take on the policeman, but Dad wouldn't let her.) Jan, finally, completely unloosened and started to sing. She has a lovely voice! The new boy could play all these folk songs, and they sang and sang, and they're going to try and work up an act for Talent Day at school. Oh, everything was great; it was perfect! I don't see why Dad finally kicked them all out. It was only three o'clock. But I have a date with Sherwood tomorrow night, and the tennis boy (Dan) is coming by tomorrow afternoon to get me for tennis, and Dot says she's going to give a party next weekend, and the folks say certainly I can have another one, just as soon as they recover from this one, in maybe ten years!

Dear Diary, dear, dear Diary . . . I may not be seeing as much of you from now on.

THE ROLLING SCONES—
A COLOSSAL CATERING CAPER

JANE WILLIAMS PUGEL

Even if the dictionary doesn't agree, Flak, Flake, and Schneider know that success is spelled f-o-o-d.

Wait a minute while I dry my hands and get away from this hot stove. A woman's work, you know . . . .

There. That clam bisque can bask alone for half an hour.

You'd never believe to look at me that I am president and chairman of the board of Rolling Scones, Inc. I mean, how many presidents of boards do you discover in a kitchen? Not many, I can tell you.

But I wander. You asked a question. Let me stir this soup once more and check the oven, and I'll tell you how all this happened.

Frankie Flake, this friend of mine, started the whole thing one dark day several years ago when she signaled me to meet her after class. Urgent. I whiled away the rest of the hour wondering about that eerie look in her eye, a look which only Frankie can get — and which can mean anything.

"Listen, I need help bad," she breathed as we huddled in front of my locker cramming potato chips into our mouths from the store of edibles I always kept for the long hours between meals. "I told — hey, how old *are* these things anyway? Stale, stale, stale — Mrs. Chisholm that lives near us, that I'd help her with a dinner party tonight. Hand me that wiener. I must have been out of my mind when I said I'd do it. I can't cook. Never even get into the kitchen. Having nine sisters has its drawbacks, let me tell you. Are you out of catsup? Ought to keep a list.

"I told her I'd help her in the kitchen because she has to feed her kids and get them to bed and wants someone to keep things stirred up, I guess." She paused, swallowed, and I slammed the locker door as I saw her eyes dart toward my cookies.

"What do you want me to do?"

"Come with me. I called her this morning and asked if I could bring someone along to help."

"Why me?" I asked. "Better hurry. There's the bell."

"You're my friend," Frankie muttered around the last big bite of wiener. "And you know something about cooking. Kitchens. Food."

"You don't do so bad in that department yourself."

"Eating, yes. Cooking, no."

We arrived at Chisholm's at five. We had decided to wear neat white blouses and dark skirts. We thought little white aprons would look nice but neither of us had one. "You know," Frankie had said, "if we look the part it might make her feel better." Somehow I felt the right note of confidence was missing in Frankie's attitude. . . .

"You can start by making some radish flowers, Frankie," Mrs. Chisholm said, tossing some bunches of radishes on the counter and taking me into the dining room to explain how she wanted the table set. Frankie looked stunned.

Later I ducked into the kitchen for silverware. There was poor Frankie crouched over the counter with lots of little objects in front of her. I peered and saw that she had taken the radishes, still replete with dirt, stems, and leaves, and stuck toothpicks into the bottoms of them. "I thought they might look like flower stems," she whispered hoarsely. Even this much effort had resulted in a bleeding finger, I noticed. From a toothpick? A radish leaf?

"Look," I said, handing her a bandage, "go in and put a fork on the left and a knife on the right. Each place." It would be easier to do the radishes myself than try to explain it to Frankie.

"Fork, left. Knife, right," she repeated as I dived into the mess on the counter and tried to recall the lesson in the art of making radish flowers which we'd had in Home Ec one day when all the fuses blew.

"Fork, left, fork left," Frankie muttered to herself as she catapulted through the swinging door into the dining room — nearly decapitating Mr. Chisholm, who had just come home from the office.

We helped him to his feet, picked up his papers, the flowers he had brought, his hat, his attaché case, his coat, the newspaper. He seemed rather preoccupied. Finally he spoke.

"Who . . . are . . . you?" he said slowly. I

thought he sounded dangerous. Frankie cleared her throat.

"Your wife, Mrs. Chisholm . . ."

"I know her name."

"Hired us. To help. Get dinner. To stir things."

"To stir things."

"To make radish flowers," I gulped.

"To make radish flowers."

"To put forks on left," Frankie whispered. "Your wife — "

"Mrs. Chisholm," he sighed. He took a deep breath, closed his eyes and opened them again and said, "You must have names."

"Oh, yes," I said. "Oh, yes indeed." I swallowed.

I should tell you at this point that the reason I know Frankie so well is alphabetical. We're always assigned adjoining places. I mean, her name is Flake, and you're not going to believe it, but mine is Flak. That's all right. No one does. Hold on while I slip these rolls out of the oven. Nice. They're one of our specialties.

"We are Frankie Flake and Frannie Flak, Sir."

Mr. Chisholm just stood there holding all those papers and odds and ends bunched up tight against his chest. Finally he asked in a very, very quiet voice, "Where is my wife, Mrs. Chisholm?" We pointed upstairs.

The dinner went off very well. Actually we didn't do much of the cooking, but Frankie did a surprisingly good job of table setting once she got it straightened out which side was left. I helped Mrs. Chisholm in the kitchen and she even asked me to remove dinner plates and bring in the dessert and coffee. We kept busy and Frankie found a lot to eat. Mr. Chisholm looked very wary whenever I was near him with the coffeepot. He had an ugly bruise on his forehead.

"Now if you'll just do the dishes I'll love you forever," Mrs. Chisholm said when the guests moved to the living room. "And I can tell you I'll recommend you to my friends if you're interested in this sort of job. I really enjoyed my own party! You were great!"

Something stirred in my mind. This sort of job? It had really been fun, and was a nice switch from baby-sitting. Maybe — maybe if I could learn a little more about real cooking and Frankie could manage to handle the table end of things . . .

"Fine with me," my mother said. "Sounds like a good idea. Only one thing: You've got to be *good* at this business if you're going to hire out as cooks." She thoughtfully tapped her teeth with a trowel (she was digging in her herb garden at the time) and coughed rather hard because there was quite a lot of dirt on the trowel. Finally she sneezed and said, "Prove to me you know your stuff, and you're on." Then she went in — to wash her face, I guess.

We decided to bring one more girl in on the project to put two in the kitchen and one handling mechanical details. That last would have to be Frankie because Julia Child she is not. Cathy Schneider was interested and we had our first meeting several days after the Chisholm Affair.

"We'll have to have a name," Cathy said when we had ironed out all the details. "So people will get to know us. Like — like — "

"Too Many Cooks Will Spoil the Broth?" Frankie ventured.

"No, no. A name, not an adage."

"Maybe KP, Incorporated," I said.

"Yes. Or Party Aids, or —"

"Rent-a-Maid?"

"I know," I said. "Something catchy. Something with food in it. Something like — Rolling Scones!"

Our firm was born. We elected officers and I became president and chairman of the board (only Cathy said it should be board and room), and Cathy volunteered to be treasurer since she can add and subtract quite easily. That left Frankie, who reached for another banana and said, "I'll be the rank and file."

I was never busier than I was the next few weeks. My career, you might say, was on the line. Cathy and I spent days studying cookbooks and hanging around my mother, who is actually pretty good at this sort of thing. She taught us a lot and gave us tricky food-prep jobs to do. We learned to handle fondues and sauerbraten and Jell-O and brioches and stews and roasts . . . you name it, we made it. Meanwhile Frankie was supposed to be learning plain and fancy table setting, napkin folding, and flower arranging from one of her many sisters.

We finally felt ready to put a small ad in the neighborhood paper:

ROLLING SCONES, INC., LTD.

Flak, Flake & Schneider

Catering — Mother's Helpers

We listed rates and phone numbers, then crossed our fingers and waited. A week later Frankie's excited voice came over the phone, "We made it! We got a job!"

A Mrs. Martin requested our help at a Sunday morning brunch. She wanted us to plan the menu, cook the meal, carry it there, serve, and clean up.

My hair stood on end but I hung up and tooled toward the cookbooks and mother.

"Creamed eggs over toast points?" Mother said later. "Yes, that sounds lovely." She tapped her teeth thoughtfully with an egg beater. (She had been making a cake.) She's always had this thing about tapping her teeth when she thinks. She wiped her chin carefully, then went on, "Broiled Canadian bacon, chilled melon balls." She nodded. "Yes, it sounds good to me, Frannie. Smart to keep it simple."

To make a long story (which seems to be growing longer by the minute, and I'm afraid I may have let my soup suffer — no, it's thriving) short, the brunch was a great success and we got two more jobs on the spot. In the next few months, we worked brunches, two major dinner parties, three midnight buffets (Frankie went to sleep at each one), and a Saturday bridge luncheon for thirteen million ladies. Our reputation was booming.

"Frannie? A Mrs. Chisholm called me," Cathy's voice came over the telephone. "She needs a dinner done the 19th. Says you and Frankie have been there before."

"Oh, my, yes," I said, remembering our first cater caper. I wondered if that lump on Mr. Chisholm's forehead had ever gone down. "Yes, we know them."

"She says this is an extra special occasion yet," Cathy continued. "Dinner and the works. Okay?"

"Okay by me. The 19th is free." I just didn't feel enthusiastic. It seemed like a bad omen, but a job is a job. I talked to Mrs. Chisholm, got the particulars, and Flak, Flake, and Schneider showed up at the proper time in brand new white aprons with monogrammed pockets. Frankie finished a candy bar, bologna sandwich, and a bottle of ice water (she was on a diet), and we got to work.

"It's Harry's big boss," Mrs. Chisholm told us as we started dinner preparations. "Top man from New York. He's deciding the fate of the local office this week; they're thinking of closing it. And they just can't! Harry has spent the past week selling Mr. Van Welles on the great future of this town. I have to do my part tonight." She rattled on in a worried way and finally went upstairs to put the children to bed and get herself dressed. Cathy and I fell to, on endive and shrimp veins and things like that; Frankie bustled (but carefully) in and out of that lethal door.

If my memory serves — oh, hold on. Mustn't let that roux get brown. Ah, there. Nice and easy does it — things began to fall apart about 5:50 P.M. At which time there was what I can best describe as a Soggy, Creaking, Crashing, Sloshing Sound. Before our unbelieving eyes, the kitchen ceiling collapsed in slow motion, bringing with it wallpaper, rubber ducks, tile, plaster, and gallons of hot water. Shrieks sounded from above, and we three girls stood stock still as water sloshed, lights went out, and the pots on the range sizzled and overflowed.

"Did you notice something?" Frankie whispered.

That brought us to life.

"Get upstairs, quick!" Cathy told her. "Frannie, get mops. Pick up plaster. I'll throw the main switch!" and she went off in search of the fuse box. I began to move and Frankie began to shout from upstairs that Mrs. Chisholm was hurt.

"I'm so sorry," she moaned. She was sitting in

the upstairs hall near the bathroom door in a pool of water. "Teddy left the bath water running — for hours, from the looks of things. I opened the door and water came pouring out. I guess it soaked the plaster and then everything went. I slipped and twisted my ankle."

Cathy barked a few more orders. I helped Mrs. Chisholm to her bed, Frankie herded the three children into a bedroom and telephoned one of her nine sisters to come and baby-sit for them for the evening. We calmed Mrs. Chisholm down about the big dinner.

"The mail will go through!" I said. "Or would you believe we have not yet begun to fight?"

We huddled and hatched battle plans. Frankie got on the phone again and started lining up remaining sisters for jobs. I began a list of things to do. Cathy worked on an emergency menu. We had an hour and a half before the Van Welleses were to arrive. The Chisholms' future was in the hands of the Rolling Scones.

I was in the kitchen a little later, working by the light of a gas camp lantern one of the numerous Flakes had brought. I had things brewing and simmering on two camp stoves another of the numerous Flakes had brought. Those Flakes are good people to have on your side.

"What . . . are . . . you . . . doing?" growled a deep, familiar voice behind me.

I whirled around, knocking a bowl to the floor. Mr. Chisholm stood staring at me as if he were having a bad dream. He clutched his coat, hat, and case to his chest. Before I could say anything he continued. "YOU. Don't tell me Snipp, Snapp, and

90

Snurr are at it again." His eyes traveled to the gaping hole in the ceiling, wet piles of debris on the floor, gas lamps, camp stoves, wet mops, and broken bowl. He leaned against the wall and whimpered, "My big night . . ."

"Your wife — " I began.

"I know. I know. Mrs. Chisholm."

" — has been hurt," I snapped angrily. "Don't just stand there. Go up and help her get dressed, for goodness sake. You're in my way!"

Well, once again to make a long story short, a very lovely dinner, lit entirely by candlelight, fireplace light, and our glistening red faces, was served in the Chisholm home that evening. Mrs. Chisholm looked very nice hopping around on one foot and she managed to play the gracious hostess through clenched teeth. Mr. Chisholm seemed to make sense whenever he spoke, and the Van Welleses — well, I never saw two people enjoy themselves more! They loved the candlelight (never knowing the reason for it) and the chafing dish of fondue on the table. They joyfully speared cubes of French bread on the long forks which an unnamed Flake had delivered to the back door only moments before. I even heard Mr. Van Welles saying he had not spent such a relaxing, *unique* evening in years. I think Mr. Chisholm moaned.

I telephoned Mother when it was time for her to bring the ice cream from our own freezer, due to the melting tendencies of Chisholms'. There was a long pause and Mother began to cough. I knew that she had tapped her teeth thoughtfully and I could only wonder what it was this time.

"Ugh!" she said. "I'm making a meat loaf. Well,

anyway, I'll bring some cherries and brandy and you can light it for Cherries Jubilee. Should fit right into your flame theme."

She did, we did, Frankie burned only three fingers carrying it in, and it was a truly glorious finale. Mr. Van Welles even cheered! Mr. Chisholm smiled. And Cathy and I and about seven or eight Flakes kept things pumped up, mopped up, and fired up in the kitchen. I doubt that such a crew will ever be gathered together again in our small city.

Well. That's it. That's the story. Mr. Chisholm not only kept his job, but a few months later he was transferred to a key vice-presidency of the firm here in New York. Vice president in charge of *ideas*. I think he still feels a little funny around us, though. He still clutches his newspaper tightly when he sees us, as if he were expecting something horrible to happen.

Which finally answers your question: how a mere girl like me happens to be cooking a meal in an elegant Manhattan townhouse. We are all three in college now, we Scones, working ourselves through — *you know how* (over a hot stove, that's how). But the Chisholms regularly fly Flak, Flake, and Schneider to New York when he wants an extra special catering job done. As he said, we put him where he is today when he was, in his phrase, *powerless*. And he feels we give him *ideas*.

So — thanks for delivering the meat, Joe. Just put it on the table there. My partners call; the aspic awaits. I must fly. Frannie Flak must get back to work.

THE ONLOOKER

ELIZABETH ALLEN

Linda feels content with Rod. He brings out a special Linda that hardly anyone knows. But can they get beyond the barrier he has put between them?

Linda walked down the hall of the hotel with her mother and stepfather. Her smile felt as though it had been applied to her face like the wrong kind of makeup. She should never have come along on this trip. It was, of course, a chance to see Europe, but she felt too much like a third wheel, an onlooker. She knew she would be glad to get back to college.

"The Tyrol has been the icing on the cake, Henry," her mother said as they sat down together in the dining room. She turned to Linda. "Haven't we seen some beautiful things, dear?"

Linda shook her hair back over her shoulders and nodded. *But it isn't enough, to see beautiful things.*

"The whole trip has been marvelous," she said very quickly, hoping that her voice sounded convincing. Neither her mother nor Henry must know that she was tired of being a spectator, that she wanted something to happen to *her*. She tried to convince herself that she was overreacting. It was not so terrible to be in Europe with her mother and stepfather. Mom was fine, as always, and Henry certainly tried.

It was not even so terrible to be in this odd situation, with both parents divorced and remarried. Certainly life with her quiet father and dominating mother had been no picnic — especially during their long and omnious silences. But it had been a life she'd been used to, had found her place in; now, really, she had no place. A kind of shadow bound and circumscribed her.

"Hi, Rochester." A boy with a shock of dark hair passed their table.

"Hello, Scarsdale," said Linda.

Her mother looked pleased. "Linda's not as shy as she seems, Henry! She has a beau."

"He is *not* my beau," Linda whispered. Her eyes followed the boy as he made his way toward the table of students across the room. They had just happened to be in several places with Linda and her parents this summer, and the boy from Scarsdale had become the brightest spot in her life. But he was just a mica-speck — not even a real spark.

"I'd certainly call him an admirer of yours," said Henry.

Linda felt that an explanation was necessary. "We've just happened to run into each other a couple of times," she said. "We talked for a few minutes at the Tivoli Gardens. He told me that he was from Scarsdale, and I told him I was from Rochester."

Her mother nodded impatiently and began discussing a shopping expedition to Innsbruck.

Linda was free for a moment to think about Scarsdale, whose real name, he had told her, was Roderick Laird. She had seen him not only at Copenhagen, in the Tivoli Gardens (he had bought her a piece of pastry), but in Heidelberg, where he had taken her to the Roten Oxen for a beer, and then up to the top of the hill to see the old castle in the moonlight. They had also run into each other in the Louvre in Paris, in front of a painting of Salome with the head of John the Baptist.

"Rochester," he had said, not looking at her, "dig that crazy dessert."

"Glug," she had answered.

"I like your response, Rochester. It's brief, understated, and to the point."

She had nodded and they walked on and stopped before an enormous painting by Rubens.

"This Rubens will never catch on," he had said. "Is he new?" But he had added, "Wow, what flesh tones."

"His girls do have a problem, though," she'd told him. "Don't they know about Metrecal?"

"I doubt it. Well, I've got to see some old church down the street. Dig you later, Rochester."

"What are you giggling about, dear?" her mother asked her, from across the table.

"Oh, nothing, really," Linda said.

A blast of laughter came from the students' table. Henry shuddered slightly; he hated noise.

"You ought to ask that nice young man to eat with *us*, Linda," said her mother. "He has a sensitive face, in spite of that awful hair."

"I don't think that's a very good idea, Mom." Scarsdale was the only part of this summer that was hers alone. There was a flicker there that could so easily be darkened.

"Haven't I seen him out in the fields, sketching?" asked Henry. "Or walking about, alone?"

That was another thing about Scarsdale. He was traveling with a group, but he was usually alone. Every time she had run into him, in their oddly coincidental meetings, he had been alone. And yet he did not seem like the loner type. It was puzzling. It was also puzzling to Linda that, although Scarsdale always seemed pleased to see her, he never made any real effort to see her again.

"That blue sweater does something for you, Linda," said her mother. "It brings out the blue in your eyes."

"Thank you," said Linda, who had decided the same thing that morning as she dressed. Was it because of him that she had put on her best sweater and brushed her hair until it shone?

Breakfast was over. They rose and left the dining room as Linda's mother continued to discuss the shopping expedition. It was their last day here, and she had to get a few things. Linda explained quickly that she really wanted to do some exploring alone, waved, and left them.

Mom would be all right. She and Henry had found each other with great delight — a discarded divorcee, an aging widower — had married and were happy.

I should find someone myself, Linda had thought. But she hadn't. Her frequent trips home during the divorce had kept her from getting into the swing of college life. She had friends, she went to parties, but that was it. Nothing exciting.

She went to the terrace to stare at green fields and white peaks. It was almost too beautiful to believe.

"Hey, Roch."

She turned and smiled.

"Please don't call me Roch," she said. "It makes me feel like some kind of bug."

"Okay. *Rochester*, if you want to be formal. What do you think of all this?" He waved a hand toward the snow-covered mountains.

"Well . . ." She hesitated. "It would be nice if any of it were real."

"Right. Do you think they use mirrors, or is it a backdrop?"

"It *can't* be canvas, Scarsdale. Canvas would blow in the wind. I go for the mirror theory."

He nodded, then spoke abruptly. "Well, I must split. Dig you later."

That was that. Finis.

If she had had any hopes that he would ask her to go sketching with him, or even for a walk. . . But she'd had no such hopes, really. Linda went to her room to get her purse and a pad of paper. She touched her lips with gloss and tied a pale pink scarf over her hair. *That's me. Pale pink. Except when I'm with that boy. He says something goofy; I say something goofy. He brings out the Linda hardly anyone knows — the me my roommates know, the me that some of my teachers know. I wish. . . .*

Roderick Laird, she thought, walking out of the hotel and up the slope. Strange boy. And that name; where had she heard it before? But she hadn't heard the name. She had seen it. She had seen it signed on the cover design of a college magazine. No wonder he sat in a field and worked. She sketched a little for fun, but he had worked at it.

He was sitting in a field near the path. Maybe on her way back, if he was still there, she would try talking to him. He might be finished by then.

Linda tried to do some sketching herself. She wanted to catch a few things merely as mementos — the tiny village with its spire, the roadside crucifix, or those children who sometimes passed as these two towheads were passing her now.

"Grüss Gott," they said shyly.

"Grease spot," she answered. She had found that they looked more pleased when she said "Grease spot" than when she tried "Grüss Gott"; apparently that got the sound better. Oh, to draw those two! She sat down on a rock and worked for awhile, but her drawings did not please her.

Linda continued up the trail. At the next village she lunched on sun-warmed strawberries and cream, and thought more about Scarsdale. She was definitely going to approach him on the way back. She might even ask if she could see what he had done that day. What harm could it do?

It was at that moment that she heard the students talking as they swarmed around a nearby table. Talking . . . about Roderick Laird! Rod. They meant Scarsdale.

"Getting fed up with his glooms . . . have to beg him to go anywhere with us . . . The guy's a drag . . . Yeah, man, but when you remember what happened to him . . ."

Linda hurried away. She did not want to hear what had happened. She could have asked. . . . No. No, of course not. She hated people who snooped around finding out about other people. She would not ask or even listen. Oh, but what could it have been? He seemed so casual and unconcerned. But, of course — when you were hurt you *did* appear casual and unconcerned. Even her mother, during the worst days of the divorce — it had never occurred to her mother that her father would really leave home — had risen at her usual time, put on fresh clothes and makeup, gone out on errands.

Perhaps Scarsdale's parents were divorced too. It could hit a boy very hard. *Something* had happened.

The air had its usual luminosity, and waterfalls were all around her, but Linda noticed nothing as she went back down the trail. *How obtuse I am. Why hadn't I sensed the pain?*

He had changed his position but was still out on a slope, sketching. Linda saw him; he was nearer the mountain path than before. Scarsdale is intelligent, she thought. He is using his talent to help him forget.

She walked faster. She had given up her idea of speaking to him on the way back to the hotel. He seemed to want to be by himself.

"Hey, *Rochester!*"

She stopped. "Hello, Scarsdale."

"Wait up. I'll go back with you."

"All right." *What do I do now?*

She waited as he gathered his things together and came toward her.

"Have any luck?" he asked. He was looking at her sketch pad.

"No. I've tried and tried to catch the village with the spire, and those children you see, and the crucifix by the trail, but it all seems to come out in technicolor."

He laughed. "I've had the same trouble myself."

"I'd love to see your work," she said boldly.

After all, other people were bold. She couldn't go on being quiet little Linda all her life. And maybe, no matter what had happened to Scarsdale, he'd welcome a new friend.

"You want to see my work? Well . . ."

He handed her a sheaf of papers. There were the sketches she had wanted to do herself and could not — mountain children in their Hansel and Gretel clothes, a quick study of the village, the crucifix by the trail. In a few strokes he had caught an essence, a feeling; his skill had given rawboned strength to what might have been too pretty and stereotyped.

"Oh!" she gasped.

"Your brevity and acumen stagger me. You have what might be called the one-syllable approach to criticism."

"These are so *good!*"

"If you really like them, Rochester, I'll give you one."

"Do you mean it? Are you sure? . . ."

"Of course I'm sure. An original Roderick Laird just for you."

She hardly heard him. She was in a whirl of indecision because she liked them all.

"The children," she decided finally.

He handed her the drawing.

"I think you're really good."

He smiled a very slight smile, but she could see that he was pleased.

"I'm actually interested in design, but I like to try everything," he said. "I definitely want to do some illustration some time."

They started down the path.

He likes me, Linda thought. You could always tell when a boy liked you. Yet, even now, as they walked along together and he helped her over a rough place on the trail, there was a reticence about him, a kind of holding back. It wasn't shyness (she knew all about *that!*). It was the dusk-colored quietness of someone who had been hurt.

They reached the hotel and went in together. Linda stopped at the hotel desk for her key, and was given a message from her mother.

We ran into some interesting people and have decided to stay in Innsbruck for dinner. We'll be back early.

"Not bad news, I hope?" Scarsdale was standing beside her.

"Oh no. My mother and stepfather won't be here for dinner. That's all."

She stuck the note in her purse, thinking, as she did so, that it would be nice if Scarsdale would ask her to sit with him at dinner tonight. Or, better yet, to go down to the little village pub.

Well, why don't I ask him? What have I got to lose? It was her last day here. It was almost her last day in Europe. They were starting for home in the morning.

"Oh, uh, Scarsdale . . ."

The moment she started she knew that this was a wrong move. To ask a boy for a date, or even hint at it, was completely out of character for her. Yet she went right on. She couldn't seem to stop. *After all, he must enjoy my company or he wouldn't be with me now.*

"I seem to be an orphan for the evening," she was saying. "And I've been dying to take in that little pub."

He had turned and was meeting her gaze. His eyes were wary.

Mistake. Mistake.

"Sorry, Rochester. Some of us had made plans. . . ."

"I see," she said softly.

"Wait a minute. Rochester!"

She was not, thank heaven, bursting into girlish tears and dashing off. She was too grown-up for that.

"I've got some phone calls to make," she said, smoothly. "Thank you again for the drawing."

She managed to get out of the lobby and down the hall without running. She went into her room, shut the door, put the drawing into her own portfolio, and then stood there and braced herself.

She had fallen into the typical shy-girl-trying-to-be-less-shy trap. In seeking to overcome her diffidence, she had overplayed her hand. It was so often the shrinking-violet type who did something really stupid.

Maybe, she thought, he had been about to ask *me* out to dinner. There had been a little flicker, a very faint one, between us. I might have gotten to know him better if I hadn't pushed.

The next morning Linda went out onto the terrace of the hotel directly after breakfast. She wanted one last look at the mountains.

"Hi, Roch," said a voice.

She jumped.

"Don't call me Roch," she said. "It makes me sound like a . . ."

"I know," he said hastily. "Sorry, Rochester."

She hadn't expected to see him again, but there he was. She sat down on a railing and stared very hard at the mountains.

"Rochester, are you leaving today? I saw your stepfather loading up his car this morning."

"Today," she said.

Scarsdale could go jump off an Alp, for all she cared.

She heard a heavy sigh.

"I don't suppose there's a chance of our meeting in England," he said. "We're off for Stratford tomorrow." And he sat down beside her.

"They tell me some cat who wrote plays used to live in this Stratford," he said. "It's on a river."

Somewhat to her horror, Linda found that she was smiling. She couldn't help it. She even wished that she were going to Stratford. She could just see this boy coming up to her in the theater during intermission and saying that *Hamlet* was a nice little play and all that, but too full of famous quotations.

I'm going to *miss* him, she thought.

"I'm sorry about last night." His tone had changed.

"Forget it."

"I won't be able to. Ever."

She was so startled by his intensity that she turned and looked directly into his face. She liked his face. She had liked it ever since that night at the Tivoli Gardens.

"Linda," he said.

So she was suddenly "Linda."

"Let me fill you in on a little matter, Linda. I have recently undergone a mildly traumatic experience."

"I thought that maybe you had."

"I was supposed to take part in a wedding ceremony in June. In fact, I was cast in a leading role. But two days before the wedding the bride decided she didn't want to marry a guy still in design school."

"Oh, no!"

"Oh, yes. Mind you, we wouldn't have been living in an attic; I'd had a slight windfall. It was my plan to be an artist that she objected to. She did say that if I'd be sensible and go into Daddy's firm she'd reconsider."

"And what did you say?"

"My words were harsh. In fact, much too harsh to repeat."

"It's all dreadful."

"Well, it was, rather. And the episode has made me rather poor company, my friends tell me. It has also caused me to avoid being in the vicinity of chicks — even pretty ones with a wild rose bloom in their cheeks."

Bloom in their cheeks. Wild rose bloom in their cheeks.

"When I realized that I might not see you again,

Linda, I was horrified. It suddenly occurred to me that the only real damage What's-Her-Face had done was to turn me into such a grouch that I would lose a chance with you."

"You're not a grouch," she said.

"I'll try not to be, Linda. I have a brother who goes to a technical school in Rochester. I plan to visit him often this year. Level with me. Are you engaged or married or anything?"

"Now, let me *think*. . . ."

"Roch!"

"No engagement, no husband," she said hastily. "A slight case of divorce in the family left me mildly traumatized, and I haven't led what you'd call an active social life."

"I see." He was getting out a pad of paper. "Please put your address and phone number and everything here, and I'll give you mine."

She didn't know why her hands were shaking. Ridiculous. His were shaking too, she noticed. And the way he was looking at her!

"We may have to take the situation slowly and let it build," she said.

"Would you say that conditions were favorable?"

"Most favorable."

"I will see you in exactly two weeks, Linda. And you'll find a letter from me when you get home."

"Wonderful."

"Lin-*da!*" her mother was calling from the hotel.

It was time to leave. He had not kissed her, or even reached for her hand, but she could feel his presence.

"Good-bye for now," he whispered.

She didn't say good-bye.

WHICH IS THE WAY TO WHERE?

PAT LAWLER

Friends Lucy has grown up with now have positive goals and she is the only indecisive one. When, if ever, will she discover the right direction for her life?

Lucy Stone stood at the window and watched the wind come racing across the yard pushing the rain in front of it. In the gutters, water foamed, and the sky was a sodden gray. A bleak Monday in May, and she was nobody in particular and had a final in senior English.

She saw Jeff's car come scooting down the street, churning through water like a motorboat — Jeff Andrews, who wanted to marry her. Lucy pulled on her slicker, tugged the sou'wester over her long, dark hair, and called good-bye to her mother in the kitchen.

In the driveway, Jeff leaned across to open the car door for her. "Hi," they said to each other,

106

and Jeff backed the car out and headed down the street.

"Have you decided?" Jeff's eyes were on the road, intent on driving and yet waiting for her answer.

"I — I don't know," she faltered, and Jeff gave her a quick sideways glance.

"I have to know, Lucy — so I can make plans for housing at school next fall."

"It's only May," she said.

"I can't wait till the last minute."

She looked at her hands in her lap, "I don't want to get married yet, Jeff."

"But this summer . . ." His hand touched her shoulder, and it made her tremble as it always did when he touched her or kissed her. But trembling — was that enough for a lifetime? I don't know, she thought miserably, I don't know about anything.

"We could get married this summer," he said, "and you could get a job while I go through school."

Jeff was going to be an engineer; it was almost a sure thing that he'd get a scholarship. He was a fine student, level-headed, and capable of drawing up his life's plan like a set of blueprints.

"But I'm supposed to go to school too," she reminded him, "at Colorado State."

He shook his head, "I honestly can't see why you want to go to college at all, Lucy. Why do you need a degree? It isn't as if you want to be anything in particular."

But I do, she protested silently. I do want to be something in particular. But what? How would she ever know? When was she going to find out?

They rode the rest of the way to school in silence except for the swoosh of the windshield wipers as they scraped holes in the rain.

At school, Jeff stopped to let Lucy out at the front entrance.

"See you at lunch?" she asked, knowing he was angry with her, not wanting him to be.

"Have to go to a Senior Day meeting."

"Have they decided definitely not to have the prom?"

"We're going to get a vote tomorrow in Assembly," he said, "but I don't think anybody will go for it. Nobody wants to spend fifty bucks on that kind of stuff these days — tux and corsage, the whole bit. A prom is kind of . . ."

"An anachronism," she suggested.

"Yeah, you know."

She knew. Suddenly the world of war and riots was very close, and a prom seemed out of place. She thought of the dress she'd planned to buy. Maybe she was an anachronism herself.

"Hey, did you know the Dempsey twins enlisted in the Marines?" It was the same subject from a different direction.

There were others in the senior class getting their service stint over with as soon as they graduated. Most would wait until they were drafted. Some said they wouldn't go even then. Jeff was in the Naval Reserve and would get a commission when he graduated from college. His life plan prudently allowed time out for war.

"We'd have four years," he spoke of this now, "before I'd have to go. Come on, Lucy, let's get married in July."

And then in four years, when he went off to the Navy, what would she do without him?

"I just don't know, Jeff." And she opened the car door and got out quickly before he could ask her again.

Melanie Brent and Laura Clark were waiting for Lucy at her locker as they were each morning.

"Guess what?" It was Melanie who, typically, started talking without even a greeting. Melanie, who wanted to be an actress and looked like one already, with long, silky hair and tiny golden earrings in pierced ears. "I got it, Lucy, the summer stock in Maine! Isn't that fantastic?"

"Melanie! Really? How absolutely great!" I am glad for her, thought Lucy, of course I am.

"I just found out about it last night. I tried to call you, but your phone was busy for hours."

"Talking to Jeff," Lucy told her.

"Oh, yeah," Melanie made a face, her pretty mouth turned down. "I hope you're not going to do something stupid like getting married as soon as you graduate."

"Of course," Laura leaped into the conversation, "there's nothing wrong with marriage. Every woman should have a home and family someday. But you should get your degree first. That's what I'm going to do. Then I'll teach for a year or two before I get married."

"Oh, Laura," Melanie moaned, "you make it sound so deadly." She turned to Lucy then, "How about you, Lucy? Have you decided what you're going to do yet? Assuming, of course," she added with a sideways wink at Laura, "that you don't get married."

Lucy shrugged her shoulders and began to put

her things away in the locker. She didn't want to talk about what she was going to do — because she didn't know. "It isn't as if you want to be anything in particular," Jeff had said. Smug, that's what he was. Melanie and Laura too — all of them were smug. And so sure of what they wanted.

"Got to get to class," Lucy said. "Big test today."

"See you this noon," sang out Melanie, but Lucy didn't answer.

She walked swiftly, not wanting anyone to catch up with her, not wanting to hear anyone else's plans. She saw familiar faces in the hall, and they looked strange to her. In her mind's eye, each face seemed to carry its own secret dream, and she felt as if she did not know any of them, really. Friends she'd grown up with now walked with brisk and purposeful stride, and Lucy was the only one out of step.

The English test was not bad at all, and Lucy thought she'd get a good grade. Not that it mattered now. All of the seniors knew that the grades they got in these last few months didn't count much one way or another. The time limit for trying hard had passed, and she hadn't even noticed when it expired. I could have gotten a scholarship, Lucy thought now. She liked school, had done well in her studies with a minimum of effort. But there hadn't been one subject she'd liked better than the rest, no signpost on the road to life. The clubs, the dances, the dating — the carefree teen years had seemed to stretch before her endlessly, and suddenly everything was different.

Somehow the morning passed and it was lunchtime. But she didn't feel like eating, not sitting with Melanie and Laura and listening to their talk.

Lucy put her books in her locker and went into the lounge to get a Coke out of the machine. There was only one other person in the lounge, a boy who stood at the Coke machine with his back to her.

There was something familiar about that broad back and the shock of blond hair that stood up in a cowlick at the crown.

"Bobby!" said Lucy, "Bobby Eilers!"

He whirled around, grinned, and, seizing her hand, said, "Lucy Stone!"

It was the same handsome face that had grinned out from sports pages all over the state three years ago, then labeled Bobby Eilers, top high school baseball player of the year. He'd been scouted all through school and picked by the Yankees when he was a senior. Lucy had been madly in love with Bobby then just as all the other girls were. That had been before Jeff, and although Bobby had never asked her for a date, sometimes he had given her a ride home or bought her a Coke at the drugstore when he saw her there. Lucy still had a scrapbook at home of his newspaper clippings. He'd had a good year on the Yankee farm team. The sportswriters talked about his potential, his future. Then Uncle Sam tapped Bobby for his army stint.

"I read in the paper last month that you were out of the service," Lucy told him, "and would be reporting for spring training."

"Yeah, well . . ." Bobby dug in his pocket and came up with some change. "Want a Coke, Lucy?" They went to sit at the table against the wall.

"Actually I'm not going to Florida for spring training."

She looked at him in surprise, "But the paper said . . ."

"That stuff," he made a gesture of dismissal. "Oh, I might still turn out to be a ballplayer. Who knows? But first I'm going to college." He corrected himself, "No, first I'm going to coach ball for the summer recreation program here. I was just down in the principal's office talking to Mr. Hawkins about it. Then in the fall I'll be going to Fort Collins, to CSU."

"That's where I'm going," Lucy said.

"You are?" His eyes held hers for a long moment, and he smiled, "That's swell." He took a swig of his Coke, "I thought about it for a long time — going to school, I mean, instead of right back to baseball. But I'm not so sure anymore what I really want."

Lucy stared at him. Why, Bobby was as confused as she was. She would have guessed that he had life all wrapped up.

"I thought I had it figured when I was eighteen," he said. "I was going to be the best baseball player in the world — or anyway in the American League." He chuckled, "Boy, I didn't know anything. I hadn't been anywhere, hadn't done much. So I went a lot of places, played a little ball, and got a free boat ride from Uncle Sam. Now what? A guy changes in three years — grows up, maybe. All of a sudden he doesn't have the same answers to the old questions."

"I haven't any answers at all," said Lucy.

"You'll find plenty," he told her, "and pretty soon you'll have more answers than questions. The trick is to match them up."

"Were you in Viet Nam?" Lucy asked him then, and his face got a closed-in look, remembering.

"Yeah, I was in 'Nam," he said briefly and appeared to study the bottle in his hand, turning it slowly. "Viet Nam — that's one of the questions."

"The world's in such a mess," Lucy said, "How does a person know what to do?"

"That's it," he said eagerly as if this were something he'd thought about for a long time, "you don't just *know*, you have to find out."

She considered his words with a growing excitement. Hadn't Bobby just given her the right answer to her own question? There was no age limit for knowing what you wanted to do, no deadline for decision. He'd said that a guy changed. A girl could change too. Even as the world turned, it changed. There would be lots of dreams before she found the right one. And love? Lucy thought of Jeff. Could she make him understand how she felt? That there could be more than one beginning, and that the happy ending doesn't come first? Jeff would be hurt, but he would rally, she knew. With a few adjustments, Jeff's life plan would proceed as scheduled.

The 12:30 P.M. bell rang, and American history class was first on her own schedule. Then, next fall, on to college and some of the answers to some of the questions.

She stood up, "I have to go to class now," and Bobby got to his feet too. "Thank you for the Coke," she said, "And . . ." She wanted to say more, but some instinct told her that this too was something to leave for the future. "See you," she called from the door.

Bobby waved a hand, "We'll make it a point."

THE ROBIN GAME

RUTH PINTER

Jack is certain he and Robin are right for each other. Now, all he has to do is let her know. . . .

The robin had to be out of its skull. I rapped on the sheet of glass we call a back door at our house. "Hey, stupid," I said, "it's only the third week of February. There's still snow on the ground. Go back to Tennessee or someplace." The robin gave me one glance and shifted its position on our grape-vine trellis. Maybe it was a way of saying, "What do *you* know?"

"Not much," I said. "You got me there."

And then I got to brooding, mostly about Robin Zimmer, a bird without feathers, but then I didn't have any feathers either, so that was all right. Robin had red hair and no freckles and all in all was kind of tough on guys. She was the best reason for my being alive I'd ever seen. There was just one problem. Most of the guys at school felt the same way — even my best friend, Benny.

The phone rang. From the back porch (where I was) to the front door (where the phone was), it was maybe 30 feet. From the Lizard's room (my younger sister, Lisa — Liza, Liz, Lizard — I worked it out one day and the name stuck) to the phone, it was at least 30 yards, downhill part of the way, true, but still three times as far. Even so I didn't have a chance. Whether I ran, walked, or crawled I couldn't get any closer to the phone than four feet. She had it down to an exact science. As soon as I hit the four-foot mark, she was there and the phone was answered.

Anyway, there I was, four feet from the phone and listening to the usual prattle that girls seem addicted to. I'd about decided the call must have been for the Lizard in the first place when she suddenly let the receiver drop into one of her sneakers on the floor. She always kicked off her shoes when she came into the house, and they usually landed under the wall phone in the hall.

"It's for you, creep."

"Thanks," I said. "It took you long enough to find out."

"Anybody calling you," she said, "deserves a little intelligent conversation for their trouble. I should send you a weekly bill for services rendered."

"Some morning when they find me completely drained of blood," I said, "I wonder if they'll catch on to you."

She wrinkled her nose and cocked her head sort of like the robin had. "That's not bad . . . considering." She flipped the receiver up out of her sneaker, caught it, and held it out to me. "Here. It's Benny."

"Hey, Ben!"

"Yeah, Dude," Benny said. "That sister of yours is something else."

"Never mind," I said. "You didn't call me to talk about Liz, did you? And how'd you make out?"

"Shot down," he said. "She's busy. And she says it as if she were sorry. Nice. But — final. Now how can a girl make you feel so high while giving you an inferiority complex?"

"Heavy thinking," I said, "but I know what you mean." I didn't have to tell Benny I was kind of relieved Robin had turned him down. Benny was now just another statistic in the Robin Game. Most of the guys in school had got there ahead of him, and there weren't too many left to play the game. Which was sort of how I'd wanted it to be right from the start.

The start was that day about the middle of fall semester when Robin had turned up at Monroe High.

The first time I saw her, Benny and I were taking a shortcut across the student parking lot after school and we saw about a ton and a half of girls piling into Emmy Novak's superheap (a '36 La Salle — beautiful).

We saw her and we both were paralyzed for about as long as it took Emmy to drive out the south exit.

"Who is *she*?" My voice squeaked a little for the first time since it started changing back in seventh grade.

Benny made a fair recovery. "What's with you?" he said. "You've known good old Emmy since kindergarten. And there was Sally Wenger and Lori Johnson and —"

"Don't try the old rip-off on me," I said. "You may be the only guy in school who knows who she is, but don't try to keep it to yourself. We'll all know by tomorrow afternoon, so you might as well tell me now."

"Oh," Benny said, "you mean the little redhead. Robin. Robin Zimmer. A transfer from Albany. About five feet four, maybe 105 pounds, won't have her phone number till tomorrow, vital statistics — nothing certain, but I'm working on it."

Benny meant it in a nice way. He has a tape-recorder memory where figures are concerned. I mean all kinds of figures, not just girls — girls were a kind of fringe benefit and a challenge to him. Added to which, Benny is irresistible to most girls. I'd always hoped some of it, whatever it is, would rub off on me, but it never had.

Next morning I got to school five minutes early and almost collided with Robin at the main door. I held it open for her and she smiled. I stood there holding the door for about a hundred other kids and ended up being late for first period.

Robin always said hi to me after that, and I usually managed to say hi back before paralysis hit. The only thing that kept me out of the deep blues was hearing about her "Thanks, but no thanks," policy as far as dating went. Obviously she knew what effect she was having on me and was waiting for me to get over it. Obviously.

So until a Monday morning in February — the Monday after the Saturday I saw that retarded bird and had to give Benny my sympathy over the phone — my contact with Robin had been limited. But now we had a replay of our first encounter, except this time after I held the door open for her,

I followed her through it. She didn't seem to be trying to get away from me, so I gave my voice a chance.

"Saw a robin Saturday morning. Made me think of you."

"Why?" she asked.

"Well, it wasn't a blue jay — and you're the only human Robin around."

She smiled, extra high voltage, and I'm not sure how the rest of the day went. That smile put me out of everything — far out.

I guess that's why I found myself in the general vicinity of Robin's locker after last period. The only reason I could possibly have had for being in that part of the building was to read the bulletin board. So I read the bulletin board. Thirty-seven students owed library fines. Turnabout (a girl asks boy dance) was coming up. The Marine Corps wanted me — or anybody who could read the poster. The Drama Club was coming on strong with *Camelot*. (They'd really wanted to do *Hair*, but . . .)

"Boo!" Two inches from my left ear. I just about climbed the board. It was the Lizard.

"Oh, you're it," I said. "The real thing. Cyanide on legs."

The big smile on her face kind of melted off and for a second she really looked hurt. But before I had time to brood about it I realized Robin was with her. My face started glowing like a boiled tomato, but I got a word out.

"Hi," I said.

"Hi," she said.

Liz had disappeared.

"I didn't know you knew Liz," I said.

"Well, why not?" Robin said. "She's got a lot going for her and she's really sweet."

"Liz? My sister?"

Robin didn't have a chance to do more than look puzzled. Benny showed up. He cut me out in two seconds flat, and I did my own version of the Lizard's disappearing act.

Now why hadn't I left school at 3:01 P.M. the way I usually did? Four days later I still didn't have an answer, but I'd perfected my shaving frown in the bathroom mirror. The Lizard caught me at it. Who locks the bathroom door for shaving?

"You could try blacking out the mirror," she said, "then maybe it wouldn't hurt you so much."

"Run away," I said. "Haight-Asbury, Greenwich Village, any old place. But before you go, how come you know Robin Zimmer?"

The Liz chewed her lower lip awhile. I'd about decided she wasn't going to answer me when she said, "French Club. Jack?"

"Yeah?"

"If I asked Benny to Turnabout, do you think he'd go?"

I shouldn't have, but I had to laugh. So Liz took off for her room, crying. I felt as if I'd been pushed into an icy shower, but what had she expected from me? Encouragement? Benny — and the Lizard? No. If she had to be hurt, then now was the best time.

There was a dance at the Teen House tonight. There was a dance every Friday night. I didn't usually go, but, but, but — the Robin Game. Benny had tipped me off to another side of the game. Robin never missed a dance. But would any guy ever get to give her a lift home afterward? As for the dances themselves, standard procedure was for guys to go and girls to go — no togetherness — and the pairing off, if any, sort of came about as the night wore on. The word was Robin would dance with anybody. She loved dancing, but none of the guys had seen her home yet.

I was out of the Robin Game, of course, what with Dad needing the car on Friday nights, and then we lived only three blocks from the Teen House.

The place was mobbed, but the group they'd imported for the night was strictly bubble gum, except for the vocalist. With a voice that ranged from a gravel bottom to a high C shriek, he took the group outasite. Without him they'd have been about as heavy as a sneeze in a hurricane.

"Hi. What's the long, long face for?" Robin's voice sounded at my side.

"Hi," I said, turning. "He's something else, and they're not even near it. I just can't get it together."

"Really? Then shouldn't I be having a good time?"

By then, of course, the paralysis had struck, so I just looked at her helplessly.

"Come on," Robin said, "dance with me." We danced.

"You see," she said, "you're having fun. So why knock it?"

I got my vocal cords unstuck long enough to say, "It's hard to explain."

"Buy me a Coke," she said. "I'll listen."

We found a small section of bar to hang our elbows on and as I ordered our Cokes, the computer in my head was analyzing all the data. First, all the girls in the house were having nice warm feelings about me because I'd taken Robin out of circulation. Second, all the guys were thinking maybe they should leave and wait for me outside. Third, Robin wasn't really interested in me, she was hung up on music; so I could relax and talk music.

"It's all in the skull," I said. "I hear what they're doing and at the same time I hear what they should be doing. Now with him," and I indicated the vocalist, "it's all in focus. What I hear and what I think I should be hearing match perfectly. With them there's a big gap in the sounds, and it bugs me."

"Are you that good?" Robin said. "Piano, guitar — what?"

I shook my head. "I'm just a collector, a listener, a music lover, whatever you want to call it."

"I'd like to hear —" she broke off. "I mean, you wouldn't mind . . . tonight if you're free . . . I'd like to hear some of the things you like."

"Sure, but it probably won't be anything you haven't heard yourself."

Robin blushed. "You wouldn't believe me."

"Try me."

"Except when I get out," she said, "like to this dance or somebody's house, I never hear anything. Mom and Dad are sweet, but music — our kind — just turns them into — well, monsters. So I don't push it. I like Mom and Dad and, anyway, nobody's perfect."

I would have argued that with her if I'd had the nerve, which I didn't, but what happened was good enough. I took Robin home.

It was my home instead of hers, but nobody had

to know that. And anyway, she'd have to get home herself eventually. If Dad got back early enough and was in a reasonable mood about me using the car . . .

I took Robin through the Doors to the Stone's country, on a flight with the Byrds and Zeppelin, to a taste of Cream and a touch of Deep Purple. I held back Steppenwolf, the late Beatles, Chicago, B.S. & T., and some of the heavier electronic stuff, Pink Floyd and Spooky Tooth, Grand Funk, and a few hard-rock splinter groups.

"The wonderful thing about it," I said, "isn't the record companies putting out all this stuff — you know they'd print anything that makes money — it's how many kids — and there must be a million of 'em — can really make it with music. I mean, that's a good thing, isn't it? Nobody ever killed a man with music, or blew up the world or did anything except make people happy."

Dad had come home a little after we did and he and Mom stayed off in the kitchen keeping themselves company. But now he joined us.

"It's late," he said, "but not too late for maybe a couple sides of Woodstock. Then I'll drive the young lady home. Might be we could get the gossips in town going again."

After they'd gone, I sat there brooding about my own father cutting me out. But it didn't get me anywhere, so I shifted to thinking over the whole Woodstock bit. It wasn't the world's best happening ever, any more than it wasn't the end of everything all-American true, red, white, and blue. What it was was history, and something more, or so Dad was saying after I first came home with the album. Then we'd gotten interrupted and never made it

122

back to that particular conversation. I was still trying to figure out what the something more was all about when Liz came down.

"Considering," she said, "you're such a creep, the music was nice. Did Robin have a good time?"

"You could have come down and joined us," I said, "it wasn't anything special."

"Anything you do," Liz said, "is what you want it to be. If it wasn't special, that's your tough luck. You're so dumb anyway; I don't know why I talk to you."

She curled up in the chair under the lamp, her hair was up and she was lost in an old robe of Dad's that was about 15 sizes too big for her. She'd started working on her nails with one of those huge sandpaper sticks and for a second I lost track of how old she was, or maybe I should say how old she wasn't. It was a funny feeling — like looking into the future. She was going to be — she *was* — a pretty girl.

"I've got to sack in," I said. "If Dad doesn't get home soon, call the cops or something."

I got to thinking before I fell asleep. When Liz had been real small, we'd had a lot of good times together. Well, I hadn't been too much bigger. There were only three years between us. Not being the same gender, naturally we'd drifted apart some as we got older. Now maybe it was time we kind of drifted together again. We were all kind of reserved in our family so far as showing affection went, but with Liz maybe that was a mistake. She'd never really been a tomboy or anything like one, and the raggy insulting banter that passed for affection between boys probably needed a little sweetening for Liz. Maybe I'd talked a little rough to her the last few years. I'd have to ease up some. Not turn mushy or anything. That kind of stuff was for the birds, in or out of the family, but ease up — she was my sister, after all.

I walked uptown next morning. What else is Saturday morning good for? I walked around the square a couple of times, then made up my mind and turned into the drugstore. What I wanted was a couple of cards. I'd soured on greeting cards one Valentine's Day way back in the third grade when May Smith had dropped mine in the teacher's wastebasket, but since Valentine's Day was safely past for another year, maybe cards would do the work for me this time. A card, after all, doesn't get paralysis of the vocal cords. I found what I wanted, then headed over to the post office and mailed them. No chickening out this time. Now I could go to the Chocolate Shop, have something hot, and brood over it awhile. By Tuesday I'd know, one way or the other. If I lived that long.

I saw Benny at the counter and took the stool next to his.

"Hi, Dude," he said.

"Yeah, team," I said.

"Some guys," he said. "Man, when you move in, you really move in."

"Benny," I said, "if I knew what you were talking about —"

"I called Robin this morning," he said. "I swallowed my pride and I called her and I said, 'C'mon, baby, ask me to Turnabout.' And you know what she said?"

"No," I said, "I don't."

"She said there was somebody else. I was sweet

124

to call and if only she could, but there was some-body else."

"Whoopee," I said.

"You said it," Benny rapped me on the arm sharply. "You don't know who the guy is, huh?"

"You said it," and I rapped him back, "for a fact."

"There was awhile there," Benny said, "I thought it might be — ha! ha! — you."

"Ha, ha," I said.

"Yeah," Benny said. "Well, I know how you feel. It's a funny thing, but I just finished that call to Robin and I got four calls myself. One, two, three, four, just like that, four invitations to Turnabout. Just like that."

"Which one did you take?"

"The first one."

"So who are you going with?"

"A girl," Benny said.

And that's the kind of morning it was. I got home in time for lunch. I told Liz between bites that I'd sounded out Benny about Turnabout and what he'd said. "Anyway, I thought you'd like to know," I said.

"Okay," Liz said, sort of emotionlessly. "Thanks."

The rest of the weekend was kind of a funny nightmare. What with wondering if Robin was just putting Benny on while putting him off, and if she wasn't, who was the bum, and then worrying about Liz (Benny must be her first real crush), the whole time was a drag. Monday wasn't any better. I didn't see Robin at all, and I wasn't sure I wanted to. I mean I wanted to, but I wasn't sure I dared. The card should have been delivered today, but she wouldn't see it till she got home after school, so tomorrow might be worse. Now if I just hadn't given in to that stupid impulse! Cards don't get paralysis of the vocal cords . . . what a bird-brain I was.

I'd barely gotten inside the front door at home when the Lizard jumped me. She got her arms around my neck and pushed her cheek against mine and sort of squealed in my ear. She was happy.

"It's been such a long time since you've really been nice to me," she said.

So I squeezed her back. There really wasn't much to her besides bones, and those were small. "How neat would that be," I said, "if I didn't like my own sister? And I was beginning to think you really believed it."

She just sort of glowed. "What movie are we going to?"

And the bottom fell out of the world. The smile froze on my face, but I didn't let it fade. "*Monterey Pop*," I said. "You know, it's not just that easy finding a movie a guy can take his sister to."

"Why do you want to take me?"

"I've got to show you off," I said. "No reason why there shouldn't be a lawnful of guys out there waiting to take you out. And once they see you having a good time, they'll be out there."

She blew me a kiss and I got into my room and dropped into my easy chair. I was glad Liz was so happy, but still, like the guy in the movie said, I blew it.

The card I picked for Robin was big and white and almost blank. What it said, in microscopic type, was "You are so beautiful." And I'd added, "How

126

about going to the movies with me Saturday?" And I'd signed it, "Jack."

The card I'd picked for Liz had a million colors on it and a kind of murky silhouette under the colors. It looked almost human. On the inside there were just a pair of eyes staring out of a black background. The card said, "So you're not beautiful and maybe you're smart not to come out in the light. I like you anyway." And I'd signed it, "Love, Jack."

I still hadn't done much except breathe now and then before I got called down to dinner. Pot roast. My spirits revived a little and it occurred to me there was a chance the card to Robin had gotten lost in the mail.

I was about to reach for a second helping when Liz asked, "Does anybody mind if Robin comes over for awhile tonight?"

"If Jack doesn't have too much homework, it should be okay," Mom said. "That's a pretty girl, that Robin."

"As long as she knows curfew's at 10 on school nights," Dad said, and coughed, "I might even drive her home again."

"What I wonder," Mom said, "is what a senior girl has in common with a freshman like you."

"French Club," Liz said, "and a really neat guy named Jack. That's what we've got in common."

I did my hot tomato imitation and wondered if I should join the beef and vegetables swimming in gravy on my plate.

"I think she really means it," Dad said, "judging by Jack's reaction there."

Liz put her hand on my shoulder, her fingers

moving just the tiniest bit. So how could I blow up or anything? I mean, the kid was just too happy.

" 'Happy Jack,' " Dad said, "now that's a song I've always liked."

And that's the way the whole meal went. They meant well, but they were dragging me to death.

Robin came just in time for dessert, and suddenly everything was okay.

"I'm sorry," she said. "I didn't mean to be so early, but meals are awfully quiet and fast at home."

"They're just the opposite here," Mom said, "and you can join us anytime. What is it you and Liz are working on so hard?"

"Just a skit," Robin said, "five minutes of light laughs. But it'll take us five months just to get it right, I'm afraid."

"That's about the right proportion of cause and effect in art," Dad said. "Don't let it get you down."

I don't know how I got into the living room, but there I was, staring out the window at a really bleak night and wondering if anybody had ever committed suicide by chewing up an LP album.

"Jack?" Very softly, right behind me.

I didn't dare turn around. "Yeah?"

"Would you go to Turnabout with me?"

So now I had to turn around.

"I — really — want you to."

"Well, sure," I said. "Maybe I shouldn't admit it, but I've been hoping — somebody — would ask me."

"I've been hoping too," Robin said, "that nobody else would ask you first. I wanted to the other

128

night, but I didn't. After I got your card today, I knew I could."

"Oh, that," I said.

"You — well, you understand," she said, "and that means a lot to me. Thanks, Jack." And then she went up to Liz's room.

Understand? Understand *what?* I must have gone to my room then and finished my homework, because when Liz dropped in about 10:15 p.m. it was all done and I was just sitting there.

"Robin said to say good night," Liz said. "We didn't want to bother you."

"It wouldn't have been a bother, exactly," I said. "I kind of like being bothered by Robin. Why she bothers with *me* is what really bothers me — mostly."

"Robin's kind of tough," Liz said, "the kind of tough that knocks everybody — guys anyway — silly. So they all come on heavy. You know, breathing hard." She giggled, "Sort of like that skunk on TV. Remember him? But gosh, Jack, you're so neat. You just treated her like a real person, not like she was some kind of living doll. So you won the Robin Game."

"Ouch," I said. "You mean all you girls knew about that?"

"Sure," Liz said. "We always knew. That's the worst of it — and the best."

FOREVER CHRISTMAS

PARM MAYER

*Mardi has always been on the receiving end of life.
Can she break out of her mold and learn to give?*

Mardi drew her long, slim legs up under her Mexican poncho and picked up the telegram that lay
unfolded on the study table.

She read the words again:

Dearest Bibs STOP Your father and I have decided that two weeks in Acapulco are far too short
so we have decided to stay another week STOP This
will of course mean that we will have to forego
Christmas at the usual time STOP But we will more
than make it up to you when we get home STOP
Better stay where you are for another week since
we've wired Julia and Wiggs and Proctor to take
a few days off STOP Mucho amor STOP Mibs
and Peter.

Just like them, she told herself. Thinking mostly
of themselves. To ease their conscience, they'd
probably have a new Torino sitting in the four-car
garage back in California, tied with a six-inch ribbon

130

in a gigantic bow and with a huge card with her name on it in gold letters.

Mardi frowned, spoiling her cover-girl face. Maybe she'd like something for Christmas besides new Torinos and fur coats and diamond-set bracelets and all that. Didn't her parents ever think of that?

All her life it had been like this. Getting, getting, getting. Never giving. Forever Christmas, she called it. The worship of material things.

It actually seemed that her parents worshipped money and the things it could buy. *Affluence* and *success*. Those were the words. Success in becoming affluent. Mardi's face darkened. As far as she was concerned, *affluence* was a dirty word.

She stood up and thumped the top of the study table with her fist. There must be some more meaningful way to live than to see how big a pile of dollars you could stash up, some solution to the crass, materialistic society in which people were living.

That was why she'd come to the small, obscure, experimental school in Outer New England, as she called it. She hoped she could latch onto some really satisfying values. Find out who she really was.

Her face brightened a little. Good thing Linda Prynne had invited her to spend Christmas at her folks' farm near Freesoil (or was it Fountain?) the moment Mardi told her about the telegram. Otherwise she'd have to stay in the empty dorm over the holidays with maybe two or three other girls who were as lost as she was.

Good old life-giving as earth Linda, with her scrubbed potato face and hoe-handling hands. A roommate you could depend on when stars fell into sawdust oblivion or an uncertain road ended in a pool of darkness.

Mardi wondered what Christmas on a farm would be like since she'd never been on anything that even vaguely resembled a farm. Quaint, like Currier and Ives cards, or like Grandma Moses paintings with their cheerful primary colors? Or boring beyond endurance?

Mr. Prynne came for the girls in his 1964 light delivery truck.

"This is my father," Linda said, indicating a lean, weather-faced man. "Dad, this is Mardi."

Mr. Prynne took off his leather glove and extended his hand. "Pleased to meet you."

Mardi put her hand in his. "Hi," she said openly.

Mr. Prynne carried the luggage and set it in the back of the truck. All three got into the cab and they started off. Scattered snowflakes were beginning to fall, hesitantly, as if uncertain of the reception they'd receive on the indifferent earth.

Mr. Prynne peered through the windshield. "Looks like we might be in for a storm spell," he observed, a comment right out of the old *Farmer's Almanac*.

The last five miles were over a rutted gravel road and the truck jounced energetically, throwing Mardi and Linda this way and that.

When they arrived, Linda's mother had supper ready, and after introductions, they all sat down to eat.

"Shall we return thanks?" her father said. Everyone bowed his head, and he composed a simple prayer. Mardi liked it, even though she didn't believe Someone Up There was listening.

"Make yourself at home," Mrs. Prynne invited and passed Mardi a platter heaped with buckwheat pancakes. Then came a platter of homemade sausages and a pitcher of "our own" maple syrup.

She looked around the table: Mr. Prynne at the head; Mrs. Prynne closest to the kitchen where more pancakes were baking on a big iron griddle; 16-year-old Beth; 15-year-old Ethan; Wendall, who was nine; the twins, Bessie and Tessie, who were six; Carol, 13; four-year-old Pearl; and Linda, who sat next to Pearl so she could cut up her pancakes. Eight children. Apparently the Prynnes didn't know about the Pill.

After supper Mr. Prynne and Ethan put on their outdoor clothes and picked up the milk pails from behind the kitchen stove and walked out.

Linda put on an old, faded mackinaw and a pair of lamb-lined boots. "We're going to the barn and milk the cows," she said to Mardi. "Want to come along?"

"Got anything I can wear?" Mardi asked.

Linda got her an old, blanket-lined jacket of Ethan's and a pair of heavy overshoes. Mardi put them on and followed Linda to the barn.

It was snowing hard now, and the wind cut their faces from out of the black rigor of the night. Inside the barn it was surprisingly warm. Hay bulged from the mangers. Cobwebs hung from the rafters and there was the smell of barn.

Mr. Prynne and Ethan and Linda each sat on a three-legged stool, against a cow's bulging side, and squirted milk from the cow into a shiny twelve-quart pail. Mardi peered around Linda's shoulder.

"So that's where milk comes from," she said. "I always thought it came from a carton."

Later Linda popped corn and everyone ate popcorn and apples and listened to carols on the radio, while a fire burned briskly in a fieldstone fireplace. Then Ethan carried in dried chunk wood from a woodshed and piled it behind the living-room stove. Mr. Prynne put two pieces inside the stove and adjusted the damper for the night, a hint that it was time to go to bed.

Mardi was to sleep with Linda and Carol. They shared an iron bed in one of the upstairs bedrooms of the old gabled farmhouse. The walls and ceilings of the room had not been plastered, and the rafters and roof boards showed aged brown in the light of the naked bulb.

"I hope you don't mind sleeping three in a bed," Linda said, and pulled the string that turned off the bulb.

A pane in one of the windows rattled and you could hear the wind tearing at the house. A few snowflakes swirled through a small crack above the bed. Prynne was probably the English word for Eskimo, Mardi told herself. She curled up against Linda, spoon fashion, who in turn curled up against Carol.

In the morning, it was still snowing but not as hard. An incredible change had come over the earth. Thick, soft topping everywhere: on the roofs, tops of fence posts, wooden fence rails, juniper bushes in front of the house, the spires of spruce trees in the backyard.

"How about going for the Christmas tree?" Carol asked. Ethan got an ax and everyone put on their outdoor things and headed for the spruce and cedar swamp at the back of the place. At the swamp, Ethan shook the snow from a white-blanketed spruce about seven feet tall. "How about this one?" he called.

"Swell!" Beth cried and the others agreed.

Mardi thought of the $50 aluminum tree Proctor put up each year at her home and didn't bother to store for another year.

That afternoon everyone helped trim the tree: handmade red and green paper chains, strings of popcorn and cranberries, shiny colored balls, candy canes, a tinfoil star at the top of the tree.

On Christmas morning, the twins passed out the presents, to be opened one at a time for all to see.

Mardi noticed that each of the Prynnes received two presents, one functional, the other symbolic of the gifts of the Magi. Linda got a sweater her mother had knitted and a chain bracelet; Carol, a new skirt and a bottle of perfume; Ethan, a pair of gloves and an inexpensive wrist watch; Wendall, trousers and a flashlight; Mr. Prynne, a booster cable for the battery of his old pickup and a bottle of shaving lotion he would never use; Mrs. Prynne, stockings and a portable electric beater.

There was a box of homemade Christmas cookies and fruitcake for Mardi, labeled "from Santa." "Now I believe in Santa Claus," she said, and she wasn't trying to be funny.

And the dinner: a huge turkey served cut up on a big platter with a turkey painted on it, mashed potatoes and giblet gravy, cranberry jelly, homemade rolls, buttered squash, plum pudding, and hard sauce. There were no canapés, no champagne.

The day lived its hours out and finally settled in the snowdrift of memory. Mardi was first to bed. Shivering, she took off her clothes and hung them on the foot posts of the iron bed and put on her nightgown. She crawled under the pile of quilts and curled up, still shivering.

What would it be like to live like this, not for a few days, but for the rest of her life? Could she endure it? Was there any virtue in being Spartan? Or was her parents' way of life right after all?

The next morning Mr. Prynne drove Mardi and Linda to the bus station, where Mardi took a bus to Boston and then a plane to Los Angeles.

Mardi laid her head back on her seat in the cabin of the jet airliner, seemingly immobile, 35,000 feet above the invisible earth. According to the stewardess, in about three hours they'd arrive in Los Angeles. Her father would be there, wearing his Santa Claus mask. Over apologetic, he would take her home in his Porsche.

As usual, her parents would have too many cocktails and would become overgenerous with their offers to get her anything she wanted as compensation for not making it home for Christmas. Or in recompense for being such lousy parents.

Would it be the same old "Forever Christmas"? Or would she rebel and say she didn't want the Torino or anything else? That she intended to spend the day alone, trying to figure it all out?

She thought of Linda and the snow-covered New England countryside. What a difference between Linda's way of life and hers! Was Linda's better simply because it was barren of luxury? Not necessarily. After all, Linda lived it because of necessity, not because of choice.

Something Linda said came back: "What I mean by Christmas is the spirit behind the glitter. The something that makes Christmas go on year after year. The love that people should have for each other, even though it sounds corny."

Mardi's face tightened. Wasn't Christmas spirit as much a myth as Santa Claus? According to the new psychology, people were incapable of loving anyone except themselves; and everything one did was for selfish reasons.

Or was it as Harvey Swados said in *A Radical's America:* "We have it within our grasp to learn with our hands and souls what it means to live well by living for others."

Maybe Linda was right. Maybe there was some kind of spirit, not necessarily the spirit of Christmas, inherent in human nature and which made it natural to love others and to want to be kind and helpful, and *unnatural* if you didn't.

Mardi thumbed through the magazine on her lap. At the bottom of an advertisement for a charity for orphans in Viet Nam was the word *GIVE* in big letters.

GIVE! Maybe that was the solution.

She remembered the cold bedroom she had slept in at the Prynnes and the heavy old quilts on the bed. Why not buy a couple of electric blankets and send them to Linda? Along with something for each of the kids. Why not?

She might even get something for her mother and father. She'd always wanted to, but they always insisted that she shouldn't. "What could you get us that we haven't already got two of?" her mother always challenged.

A new feeling came over Mardi. She, Mardi Adele Prentiss, giving instead of receiving. It was funny. Fabulously funny. So funny she laughed a little.

Anyway, it would be a beginning, and maybe she could work out the rest in the months ahead: help teach retarded children, join an organization that tried to further better racial relations.

It was time for meals, and the hostesses brought in trays. Mardi ate with more appetite than usual — something like the way she ate pancakes and sausages that night at the Prynnes.

Across the aisle, a young mother was finding it difficult to manage her baby while helping to feed her two-year-old.

Something like a crocus pushing through the ground in early spring pushed into Mardi's consciousness. She told the hostess to take her tray and bring it back later. "How about my holding the baby while you and your child eat?" she suggested to the woman.

The woman smiled and handed the baby to Mardi.

"What's her name?" Mardi asked.

"Holly," the woman said.

"That makes sense. This time of year."

"It's supposed to mean *happy*."

Mardi sat with the baby in her arms, happy in a way she'd never been before.

Soon the pilot announced, "We are beginning our descent. In approximately 15 minutes we will land in Los Angeles."

The words echoed: Los Angeles. *The angels.* Angels. Those impossible creatures you sometimes saw on Christmas cards, who went around littering the earth with legends like *Peace On Earth, Good Will Toward Men.*

Mardi quickened. Maybe they were believable after all. Maybe Christmas *could be* forever.

MY OWN THING

AUDREY LAZIER

With Doug at her side, breaking into the acting world will be easy, thinks Tracy. But she finds herself waiting all summer for that "Instant Success."

Doug once told me I had rocks in my head. "Tracy," he said, "you've got rocks in your head."

I mean, is that nice? Every girl, he claimed, wants college, romance, marriage, and babies. To which I added homework, heartbreak, bills, and dirty diapers. Don't get me wrong, I'm not knocking any sacred cows. But I have a yen for something different. And if Destiny intended to give me a push down the domestic path, I'd just have to turn around and give Destiny some of its own.

I squared off by sending out applications last March to a couple of dozen summer stock companies. Now you've got it. I groove on the acting scene.

"Can't you just see me?" I say to Doug one day

as we're lunching on the quad, "taking my curtain calls as the audience shouts 'Huzzah!' and tosses roses at my feet?"

"As long as they're roses," he smirks, "and not rotten tomatoes."

I sniff. "I've got talent."

"Yeah. By the bucketful."

He makes me nervous when he talks like that. With the mysterious intuitive sense of the female, I know I have talent. The only trouble is, I haven't really been able to put it to the test. A walk-on in the senior play hardly gave me a chance to dredge up my deepest passions. Still, it's there — a talent, God-given, I read somewhere — and who am I to quash it?

"Are you sure you don't want to chuck all this nonsense," Doug says a few days later, "and spend a lazy summer lolling on the beach?" Beaching is his bag, as witnessed by the fact that we are at this moment on the beach, he in his scarlet trunks and me swathed in a parka against the icy March winds. (Who's got rocks in whose head?)

"Youth comes and goes," I chatter. "The beach remains forever. I'll loll in my retirement."

"And how is my summer going to turn on without you around for laughs?"

I flutter my eye lashes at him. "Why, Doug. I didn't know you cared."

He rolls over with a groan. "I don't. You're just a bad habit."

I try to convince him there are plenty of other chicks around. But he lies there, propped up on his elbows, with a dull glaze over his brown eyes. I have the uneasy feeling he's flipped out, and he has. Because the next thing he says is a bombshell.

"Give me the list of those stock companies you wrote to."

My eyes pop. "You're goofing on me!"

"If you can't lick 'em, join 'em."

"Zap!" I say. "And zap again."

That's how Doug and I end up after graduation doing a season together at the Wauwepesaukee Playhouse in Indiana.

Actually, the playhouse is a huge tent covering the stage and about 150 folding chairs. Tent is the wrong word. It's really an oven. We keep the sides up in the daytime to keep the temperature down to 90.

The resident company (12 of us) lives in a big two-story wooden house, along with the director, Phil, the company manager, Joe, and a 50-year-old stringbean with gray hair who answers to the name of Cheri and cooks our meals — not with imagination so much as just pure grit.

Between the house and the tent is an old barn, replete with stale hay, mice, and an occasional bat. We don't go in there very often.

But then, we don't have time to. The breakfast gong sounds at 8 A.M., and we vibrate out of bed. Rehearsals run from nine to twelve and two to five, with performances in the evening. The bothersome thing is, I'm not rehearsing.

"You've got a part," I wail to Doug one hot morning outside the tent, "and I've got a paintbrush!"

He grins. "I'm just talented, I guess."

"Bricks!" I sputter. "The whole set is one great big brick wall. Do you know how many bricks there are?"

"How many?"

141

"I'd count them, except there isn't time. The season ends the middle of September!"

"You speak in riddles."

"You don't even speak English!"

He folds his arms and gives me a look like he's going to send me home with a note to my mother. "You're complaining."

"And why not?" I retort, making a great sweeping gesture with the paintbrush, which leaves him unimpressed but leaves a big glob of red paint in my hair. "How can I find out if I'm an actress if I'm not acting?"

"Just be glad you're here," he says dramatically, and now I know he's putting me on. "The magic of the theater . . . the smell of the greasepaint, the roar of the crowd . . ."

"Fiddle!"

After lunch I decide to abandon my paintbrush and sneak onto the screened-in rehearsal porch to watch the proceedings. A gentle breeze wafts from the lake, but to the west I see clouds gathering for a summer storm. I make myself as small as possible in an overstuffed armchair, which isn't so overstuffed anymore what with all the holes in it. Doug and my roommate, Gena, are rehearsing a love scene. She's a long-legged redhead from New York City, and I can see Doug is enjoying his work. I try to remind myself that it's their business to be convincing, but they still have the scripts in their hands and Doug is kissing her like it's the closing night of the show.

Phil interrupts them to give some direction, and when he turns back to his seat, his dark eyes fall on me.

"Tracy," he says, "have you run out of paint?"

I smile brightly. "I, ah — I thought I should get to know the play. In case anything happens to Gena, I could go on for her."

He runs a hand through his shock of black hair. "Thank you. But even if Gena were dying, we'd strap her to crutches and she would go on."

Gena is smiling; Doug is scowling. I say "Oh" and unwind out of the chair.

"If you've got nothing to do," Phil pursues, "you can go down to the lake and scrub the company's pier."

"Fink!" I say later to Doug, but he ignores me.

The following Monday the cast for the new show is announced. I learn I come on in the third act and say "Dinner is served, ma'm."

"This whole summer is turning into one big cliché," I moan to Gena over lunch.

She laughs. "You're going through what I went through my first summer." I don't doubt her, but it isn't much comfort. "And now I'm doing leads and I have an agent in New York who's prowling the casting offices for me."

That impresses me. "No kidding!"

"And it only took me five years."

That doesn't! In fact, it's a belt below the belt. "If I can't make it in two years, I'll chuck it."

"Then you'll chuck it," she grins, and she's so positive about it I'm in a blue funk the rest of the day. At five o'clock I stroll to the edge of the cliff overlooking the lake. The wind is up, and raindrops are beginning to fall. But I don't care. I put my arms around an elm and defy the elements. Lightning blazes, thunder cracks, and the rain is whipping in my face. Suddenly I'm Catherine in *Wuthering Heights*, struggling across the stormy moor looking for my abandoned lover.

That makes me feel a lot better. I resolve to retreat to the house in order to wring myself out before dinner.

In the dining room we toast the opening night of Doug's show with tomato juice. Then Doug proceeds to pack away his dinner like a boa constrictor that hasn't eaten in six months. I marvel. If it were my opening night, my stomach would be so squeezed with stage fright I couldn't poke down an olive.

The show goes well, and we celebrate afterwards with a cast party. I've got to admit I can enjoy a party even without being in the cast. As a matter of fact, the whole summer is beginning to pick up. I go to rehearsals, even if it is just for one line. But soon that situation improves, because the following week I get cast in a show where I have 10 lines in the second act. I must confess that Phil has to sit on me a little.

"Tracy," he says in a heavy voice. "You're just giving a little exposition to lead into the second act. You are not Joan of Arc burning at the stake. Okay?"

I smile gamely. "Whatever you say, Phil."

When opening night finally arrives, I have a good case of the flutters. But everything goes smoothly, and afterwards Phil gives me the nicest backhanded compliment I've ever received. He says, "You did a very nice job for someone like you."

Doug says I ought to have that engraved on a medallion and wear it around my neck. I ask him for some more good ideas.

144

The weeks gallop by. I get callouses, splinters, hammered fingernails, heat rash, mosquito bites, letters from home, not enough sleep, too many Cokes, and an occasional part.

And then finally my big break comes.

It's Monday at the breakfast table, and Phil announces the cast for the next-to-last show. "Tracy," he says with a ferocious grin on his face, "I know this will displease you but I am forced to give you you the leading role."

I let out a whoop, and the kids start tapping their forks on the water glasses. The play is called *Barefoot in the Park*, and Doug and I play the young married couple who live in New York in a walk-up apartment.

The rehearsals are a lot of fun and a lot of hard work. It's kind of funny having Doug play my husband. It gives me little flutters in the stomach sometimes. I guess Doug gets the same feeling because Sunday night after final dress, while Doug and I are taking a midnight swim in the dark still waters of the lake, he says to me, "It could be for real, this play."

"Spooky, isn't it?" I answer, treading water beside him.

"Well, I don't think it would be *that* bad."

"Why, Doug! Is that a proposal?"

He floats on his back, arms spread wide. "I'm just dropping a sounding line to see how deep the water is."

I laugh and make some witty retort, but the old flutters start up again. It's the closest I've come to an honest-to-goodness proposal, and I feel kind of funny and tender and sad at the same time.

Monday, the day of the opening, dawns bright

and hot. There are a million last-minute things to do: finish dressing the set, check over and press costumes, dust the chairs for the audience, set up the refreshment stand, sort out the tickets, pick up the programs from the printer.

I'm in a daze. My head is full of cotton, and I can't remember a single line. I keep clutching at Doug. "I can't go on! I can't!"

"Relax!"

"I'll open my mouth and no sound will come out. . . ."

"That in itself will be something worth seeing."

I make a face. "In my hour of need you are proving yourself as sturdy and stalwart as a bowl of mush."

"Tracy, my girl," he says, "you'll wow 'em! You'll give the greatest performance this side of . . . this side of . . ."

"Wauwepesaukee Lake?"

"Exactly!"

But I never have a chance to prove it. Destiny, it seems, has not lost the fight. She takes measure of me and gets off a good one.

It's five o'clock, and we idle on the porch waiting for supper, massaging tired feet and frayed nerves and watching dark clouds gather in the west.

"What a gink if it rains on my opening night," I mutter, and everyone is more or less in accord. Gena and Doug and I wander out to the edge of the cliff. Sure enough, on the far side we see a sheet of rain. It's advancing on us as inexorably as Napoleon's troops on Moscow.

"My hair!" I shriek. "It'll get ruined!"

The three of us race the wall of rain to the

house. We slam into the rehearsal porch just as the rain hits. There's such a roar and a clatter we can't hear ourselves talk. The wind shrieks around the house, rattling the windows, booming down the chimney. The rain slams to earth so densely we can't see three yards beyond the house. It's kind of exciting. In fact, it's a real gas. We're laughing and having a good old time.

And then, as abruptly as the storm arrived, it departs. We straggle out to take a look around, make sure everything's okay, that the tent is still standing, and so forth.

We all stop dead and deliver a unified gasp. It isn't.

The tent, I mean. It's lying beyond, flat on the wheat field, torn and practically bleeding. And its innards are completely demolished. The chairs are collapsed, the set is just plain gone, and the stage sags at a dismal angle. Electric wires are down. And the set props are scattered like discarded toy furniture.

It's a full five minutes before anyone makes a sound. And then it's Gena, and she's crying. That brings a little of the elixir to my eyes too. Doug puts his arm around my shoulders and gives me a squeeze.

Phil phones to have the power turned off, and then we set about to salvage what little we can. The boys move the furniture into the barn and the girls hunt and collect hand props and odds and ends.

We sit down to dinner late. Everything is kind of tepid and dried out, but none of us is hungry anyway. Then Phil gives the word.

"The show is canceled. It'll take us a week to turn the barn into a theater. Costumes and props are already rented for the last show, so we'll have to go ahead." The last show is *Gigi,* and Gena has the lead. She gives me a funny look and then fastens her eyes on her plate.

Phil turns to me and says, so warm and sincere, "I'm sorry, Tracy."

That brings the quivers to the dimple in my chin.

Later I march up to my room, plop down cross-legged on my bed, and have a good hard think. And the harder I think, the madder I get. I work my fingers to the bone just to get shot down in my big moment. Whoever said there ain't no justice ain't whistling Dixie! I'm fed up to here!

I make a decision, and the force of it propels me off the bed and into the closet where I keep my suitcase. I slam it on the bed, fling it open, and start jamming clothes in it. I'm so wrapped up in my melodramatics I don't see Doug leaning in the open doorway.

"You look like a bride running home to Mama."

I whirl on him. "You're right! When the marriage proves a fraud!"

He grins at me. "You're copping out."

"Painting bricks and building a theater in a barn is not my idea of the acting scene."

"What is?" he asks, still leaning, still grinning. "David Merrick bringing you a play on a silver platter? Jack Warner begging for a screen test?"

I draw myself up to the full height of my disheveled dignity and ignore his smart remark. "The acting scene is — is acting! Doing leads, working with good directors, being seen . . ."

148

I slam the lid shut on my suitcase, but everything is such a jumble that sleeves and toes and ribbons and garters stick out like a boxed octopus. "I'm going where the action is."

"You and about 50,000 others."

I look at Doug, at his silly grin. "Why don't you go play with the kids down the block?"

He gives a big laugh and then suddenly he grabs me and kisses me, which I think is a complete non sequitur to the subject under discussion. But since my toes are beginning to curl, I decide to let his inference wander from the premise. Besides, he never kissed Gena this way.

When at last he releases me, I sag onto the bed. I expect to see the razzle-dazzle in his eyes, but instead, he's frowning.

"You wanted to do your own thing. Well, this is it! This is part of the breaks. So what if the show doesn't open? You've got a week of rehearsals with a good director under your belt." His eyes are snapping. I've never seen him quite so sturdy and stalwart. "If you can't take the disappointments and the hard work, then you'd better shake the rocks out of your head and go to college and get married. . . ."

". . . and worry over bills and wash dirty diapers . . ."

"Right! Because right now you're a loser. And I don't want any part of a loser!" He pauses and scratches his head. "Come to think of it, though, if you're a winner, I won't get any part of you anyway." He looks at me and gives a sheepish grin.

That does it. A lump gathers in my throat. I make my decision and play the flip side. "You're absolutely right, Doug! If I have to fight disappointment, competition, the elements themselves, then by golly-gosh, I'll fight!"

Doug gives me a clap on the back. "Stout fellow!"

I surrender myself to more callouses and hammered fingernails. But not for long. Wednesday afternoon Phil pulls me aside and pours golden words into my ears until they're ringing like bells. Gena's agent has got her a part in a commercial and she's returning to New York tonight. Would I like to do Gigi?

I give him a look that gives him his answer.

It's a feverish time getting up the part in four days but it's a wonderful, soaring experience. On Monday night we make two toasts over our tomato juice — one to the new theater and one to the opening night.

I stand backstage in my skirt and middy blouse awaiting my first entrance. Doug tiptoes up and kisses my cheek.

The performance goes smoothly. I remember all my lines after all, and some of the scenes really catch fire. The audience laughs and chuckles and stays right with the show, even despite the brief but thoroughly frantic visit by a bat.

We take our curtain calls, and the warm applause swells up over the footlights. It is ambrosia in a silver goblet, and it makes me deliciously drunk. I glimpse Doug standing in the back of the house, but he's not applauding. He looks solemn and thoughtful.

Afterwards, the dressing rooms are abuzz with excitement. Some people are there, congratulating us. We're all stringing along on high C. But Doug isn't there, and suddenly it's the most important thing in the world to learn what he thinks of my performance.

The crowd thins out, and I've started taking off my makeup when he finally appears in the doorway. I rush to meet him.

"Well?"

He's looking at me, and his eyes have a new kind of shine to them.

"Well?" I say nervously, "Did you like my performance?" I know somehow that if he liked it, *really* liked it, I'd be on my way.

He nods slowly.

"And — and do I have rocks in my head?"

He shakes his head. And then he grins. "By gosh, Tracy, you *have* got talent." Then he pulls something from behind his back. "It took me awhile to find this."

I look, and then I begin to laugh. And he does the sweetest, most wonderful thing in the world — he tosses a rose at my feet.

THE IDEAL COUPLE

SUSAN INGALLS

Nina found out long ago that it was silly to play equals about love.

All of a sudden, in the midst of November, she started feeling romantic. Her heart was warm and mellow and began escaping her at odd moments. In the past year she had come to define such spells as the aura of unrequited love. Simon-and-Nina was a phrase, and she was Nina. They had never been romantic. Though they went to separate colleges (one men's and one women's, a couple of hours apart), on the weekends they were always together; she just fitted under his arm (she used to say it was her place in the world). But, Nina thought, there had certainly been very few romantic words between them. They had never even talked about whether they loved each other — the question was so incidental to their happiness.

Nina's friends thought they were the ideal couple, which made Nina smile to herself and hope Simon never heard it; she knew it would scare him.

All that week she felt strangely independent. Nina wondered if she could ever be the opposite person in all the love songs, the one who leaves. In tune with the record player she tried to sing her heart out of her mouth: *This little bird, she can fly away.* The words had a new twist; she had never been the one to leave, but the possibility was exhilarating — especially since she didn't really believe it herself. She was just playing with words and stories in her mind, the way she had done before she met Simon.

Walking down streets in her small college town, Nina found herself caught by boys' faces, wondering what they would be like, whether they would listen to her words as well as her laughter, her poetry as well as her . . . As well as her what? The balanced phrases she had been building in her mind fell apart as she admitted that Simon, after all, was the one person in the world who would listen to all her words, even the silly, wasteful ones, without impatience or sarcasm (though not usually with complete attention).

Besides, Nina wondered, mirrored on both sides by fragments of herself flashing through the long rows of car and shop windows, if any other boy did notice her, what could he see? Her face no longer lived under that sad-eyed-young-woman look it once had had. Not that it had attracted any romantic lovers, but she'd dreamed that, deepened by a few years, it might be the kind of face that was discovered, that someone would want to paint. Now she had that look so rarely, only when concentrating, that Simon, seeing it, would glance up and ask what was wrong. He had made that look a stranger to her face. Since Simon, she had curled her sun-colored hair so that the ends seemed, in the words of a friend, as if they were smiling. She had gone so far as to put on a few contented pounds. And as she edged closer to her reflection, tilting her head in consideration, she could not help grinning at herself, transforming her reassuringly again into Simon's Nina.

It was funny. Last spring, her last in prep school, she had been perfectly happy for the first time since puberty. That was because of Simon. It had really been one of those idyllic springs people make movies about. And, as if it were one of those movies, she had savored it, fully expecting it to end. But it had gone on, and this fall she was no longer so happy. It wasn't, as logic suggested, that she was tired of it or of Simon. She knew what it wasn't, but not what it was.

Was it guilt over her newfound mood that compelled Nina to announce during Simon's regular Wednesday night call, "I've been feeling romantic lately"?

Simon laughed. His soft, mumbly voice reminded her of his dimples and black curly hair, like a dark cherub. "So what have you been doing, now that you're romantic?"

"Listening to Tim Buckley records." She wondered if he would remember how she had listened to Tim Buckley and Judy Collins in the sad months before she met him, when she was still dragging out her love for Chuck Dickson. Momentarily Nina resented that Simon had never been at all jealous (before this she had enjoyed the ease with which they'd exchanged stories of former dates, like friends, never having to hide things with the coyness she detested in other couples).

But Simon obviously had no idea what she wanted him to be thinking, for there was his voice, held between her ear and one hunched shoulder, just telling her how he'd spent his day, from getting up in the morning to "So I finished a chapter of Locke and decided to call you now." Nina let the events of his day slip past her, listening instead to the familiar cadence of his voice, letting it entice her into thinking how much she liked him, waiting for him to say something nice like "I miss you" before he hung up and left her.

Somehow, when he got all itchy and wanting to hang up, she hated to let him, which was ridiculous in her new plan of being more independent-romantic, but after he'd told her good-bye a few times to get used to the way it sounded, the line was horribly empty. Nina surprised herself by crying violently into her pillow, for which she could find no excuse.

Nina was still wondering about herself Friday afternoon when she stumbled into the bus, most of her view blocked by a huge floppy hat she had grabbed as she'd rushed out of her room and pulled down over her face so it wouldn't blow off. It was Simon's favorite; he'd bought it for her in the Goodwill store. She had to tilt her head far back to see as she pushed toward the rear of the bus (away from girls who were spending their first weekends at the men's college and would want to talk about the reputations of different fraternities), bristling with notebooks she hadn't had time to pack properly, pushing her suitcase along with one foot, as though she had a limp. Tucked among her packages, Nina sang under the grumble of the bus for it to rush, rush, rush.

As they turned off the highway, Nina removed the hat, smoothed her tangled curls with her fingers, and tried to get a clear picture of her face in the darkened window as the bus slipped through an underpass. She had put on makeup this afternoon, knowing Simon didn't like it, though he probably wouldn't notice. She hadn't worn lipstick, of course (Nina wondered how anybody who ever kissed anybody could wear lipstick), but putting on some makeup was almost like getting ready for a real date. Being with Simon wasn't much like a date anymore. There was none of the elaborate preparation or the nervousness; usually there wasn't even a special place to go, just sitting in the poolroom or TV room of the fraternity house, doing a little studying, talking with his friends. She wasn't lazy about her looks, just tired of hearing Simon say, "What are you so dressed up for? You make me feel uncomfortable." Besides, most pre-football Saturday mornings she wasn't up to wearing eye makeup, and she felt rather silly slipping into the ladies' room about six P.M. and coming out differently colored. It was just once in awhile, like today, that she wanted to "dress up."

As the bus pulled to the stop and Nina saw him again, his serious wire-rimmed glasses belying the impression given by his muscular shoulders under a crimson and gold high school football jacket, her warmth of heart reached out to envelop him in her mood. The impact of that first glance set off remembrances inside her; he looked so excitingly like the first night she'd met him last February — so handsome she'd been almost frightened. He was wearing the same jeans; Nina had memorized the way they hung loosely on his hips.

"Oh, Simon," Nina said as she tumbled out of the door upon him. "Aren't you glad to see me?"

She heard a mumble of "You know," and then she was home in his safe hug. All their greetings and questions blurred those first moments together for her, now that she was close to him.

Simon looked down, touching her protectively, setting the hat back off her face, pulling up the furry collar of her coat to warm her ears. His eyes, a warm brown that lit up toward the center, were almost sentimental. "You look pretty today," he confided, "not that you don't usually look good," he rushed on, caught by the way his mind had to make conclusions, and she laughed.

Nina was so happy, following along beside him, holding hands. Their hands held together looked young and touching, as if this were a first subteen date. She wondered if there were any married people who still held hands.

Close to Simon, Nina couldn't imagine ever leaving him, nevermore to be hugged or smiled at or even ignored while he was writing a paper. He seemed so innocent of all her thoughts of dissatisfaction that when they were dissolved by his presence, she had to tell him, throwing her arms around his waist. Nina squeezed, lifting him right off the ground, and begged, "I never have to go away from you, do I?"

And Simon, so different from other boys, who would have balked or hedged or tried to be reasonable and honest, said, "Never."

Nina smiled because they both knew it didn't have anything to do with a proposal of marriage, so in her happiness she skipped as well as she could in knee boots, a fur coat, and floppy hat. Simon surprised her by joining in the skip.

First, as usual, they went to drop off her suitcase at The Willows, along a wide street lined with gangly Victorian houses, cornucopia-towers jutting out everywhere. Each week Nina picked out a house to pretend was her own, which rooms would be hers, which would be Simon's study. Today she discovered, hidden behind a tangle of dead vines and wayward bushes, a decadent mansion with a stone tower growing out of its side. "I want," she said aloud, in case he might be listening, "to live at the very top of that tower, in a round room, like a chamber in a castle. Isn't it a magnificent house, so proud and wild?"

Simon looked up from his preoccupations. "It is sort of wild, especially with that great tree in front of it; look at the twisted branches against the sky."

Nina tried to think of some further revealing statement to make about the tree but failed. She wanted to share the tree with Simon, but she couldn't do it by saying "yeah, wow" so she didn't say anything. They walked on. It was the wrong time of year to be romantic. She tried to blame it on the resemblance of the weather to February — the day was in-between — it could have been preparing for either winter or spring. She remembered a game she had made up to play with herself when she was little, pretending she was on a quiz show: They showed her a picture of the day, and she tried to guess what time of year it was. She began collecting little moments of time with all her senses and stuffing them carelessly into her memory.

"You know, I love this walk. It makes me feel like a real person, with time to notice things, not just a student."

"Ummmm."

Of course he didn't understand. Studying was Simon's favorite life, what he wanted to do forever: be a great thinker, know the truth. Nina sympathized, but she felt cooped up, always studying. There was more in life. He could see it too, if he took the trouble, but Simon was wary of going to art shows or poetry readings, purposely not artistic in that sense, as if he were afraid of such a role. "I don't know anything about . . ." he would say, till Nina got tired of asking. But it really didn't matter, she decided. She could be happy on this walk without anyone sharing it. She started singing.

Simon turned his attention toward her, squeezing her hand. "You're really in a good mood, aren't you?"

"Oh, yes, I feel like a party inside."

He frowned slightly, the frown he used when he was upset with himself. "It's too bad you have to feel this way tonight. With my hourly coming up on Tuesday I don't really think we can go out. If we want to go to the game and party tomorrow, I'll have to study."

He looked so sad and torn that Nina rushed to reassure him. "Oh, I don't care. I'm just happy *now*." Then she heard her voice turn impatient: "Why do people always think that if you're happy, it's dangerous, as if the future of being happy is being unhappy?"

Simon felt impelled to justify himself; he thought she had meant it as a personal criticism. "Nin, you know I worry like that. I can't help the way I am."

"Oh, I know. I'm not mad," she almost shouted. She wished they'd get to The Willows. What was wrong with Simon anyway? He hadn't said anything voluntarily the whole walk. "Stop it," Nina demanded.

"What?" he answered after the statement reached his consciousness in about ten seconds.

"Ignoring me."

Simon grinned to himself. "I wondered how long it would take you to get mad."

Now she was furious, glaring at him.

"I thought you said you were in a good mood," he said reasonably. "Don't ruin it."

You ruined my mood, Nina thought savagely, still glaring.

Simon tried to avoid fights. Now he carefully took the trouble to explain, "You don't have to be hurt. I never pay attention to what people say to me when I'm thinking. It's not just you that I ignore."

"You're always saying that, as if admitting your faults made them right because you're not being hypocritical. Didn't you ever think that its hypocritical to admit faults but not do anything about them?"

"Now, come on." Simon's voice revealed irritation; he was tired of this. Then he tried to change it all into a joke. "Besides, you talk so much, I have more opportunities to ignore you than I do anyone else."

Did he really think she talked a lot, when she kept half of everything to herself? "What do you mean I talk so much?"

"Well, once I had a girl who talked almost as much as you do, but then I only saw her once a month, so she had an excuse. She'd saved all those things up."

Nina saw he was still saying this jokingly, but then he always pretended things were joking when he knew they'd make her mad. And she *was* mad, and hurt, just as she had felt the day he'd told her it was too hot to hold hands. Nina stopped walking and just stood, not caring if she looked ridiculous.

By the time Simon had walked halfway down the block without even noticing, or seeming to notice, that she wasn't with him, she'd recovered enough to decide to catch up, trying to hide her heavy breathing as if she hadn't been behind, determined not to say anything.

Simon looked at her sideways to judge the seriousness of her anger, then said, "Come on, I don't want you to be mad. Let's sit down and talk about it." He pulled her over to some steps, where she sat a few feet away from him, concentrating on the splintered wood. "Don't make your shrew face," he said, and as she looked up in surprise, he moved close and held her. He tenderly brushed the curls out of her face where they had flown while she was perturbed; it was a gesture that always comforted her.

"What is my shrew face?" She had almost forgotten that he hadn't apologized.

Simon contorted his features in a way she recognized as her own, and she burst out laughing. She nestled her head into his shoulder. "Are you worried about the test?"

"I suppose. I was trying to think of an argument for civil disobedience. What would you think if I said . . ?" They started walking again, but this time together, and she had no attention for her surroundings until they were climbing up the steps of The Willows.

The Willows was demure; only a couple of rooms were rented out, and those smelled faintly of orange blossoms. How Nina had hated her weekends at Mrs. Whipple's boarding house, with six girls to a long, dormlike room and someone always climbing over your bed on the way to the bathroom. Here she had her own room, a brass bed, and lilac-sprigged wallpaper.

Nina saw a set of matched cream-colored luggage as they passed the other guest room. "Is Kim staying here this weekend?" Kim and Paul (Simon's closest friend) had known each other before she'd met Simon, but they still hadn't settled into routine — though they were officially "in love."

"Yeah, she tried that trick she has of refusing to come unless all Paul's work is already done, but in the end he talked her into it. I wouldn't have bothered."

Simon was really such a gossip, though he liked to pretend he was too intellectual and "strong-silent" to be one. Nina loved to talk with him about people: They agreed, they understood each other's emotions even if they didn't share each other's thoughts.

They agreed about Kim; they both distrusted her though they liked her — Simon because he'd dated and broken his heart (how impossible to think of him with a broken heart) over Nancy Bruce, and felt he had to warn Paul that Nancy and Kim were both the kind that make you unhappy; Nina (who had never made anyone unhappy —

which might have been why no boy had ever said he loved her) by instinct, distrustful of girls who love-talked in contradictions: I love you but . . . I need my freedom, I want to go out with other people, I want our love to be natural and spontaneous, I don't want to be tied down.

"Their love is a farce," Simon said.

"But how can they admit it?" Nina asked. "You know Paul needs someone to love – he isn't sure about his goals or school or his parents, all he has is Kim — you know how unhappy he was before he met her."

"Frankly, Nin, I don't think this is any better." He was harsh because Kim was hurting his friend.

Nina sat down on the pompon quilt, picking at the balls of fluff. "It's so sad. The only people we know who *say* they are in love, and it isn't love at all — it's a horrible fake." She pushed out her lower lip and narrowed her eyes. "People like that ruin the reputation of love. People don't *want* to be in love anymore." (*Like Simon,* her heart said; *Nancy made him want to stop loving.*)

Simon smiled at her. "What's really scary is that they've been talking marriage," he said with near-loathing. "Paul thinks if they were tied together in some way, things would be better; she wouldn't be so hung up."

"What did you tell him?"

"What could I say? I try to talk to him logically; I tell him he's letting her walk all over him with her whims. Of course, talking doesn't do any good. I could get him all straightened out in conversation a hundred times, and it would never work out with Kim. If he only went out with a girl like **you** a few times, someone to cheer him up, get him doing things instead of adding to his problems, who'd show him some simple affection — then he'd understand."

Simon smiled as if it were a compliment. Would he ever understand that she wasn't an ideal type all boys should have one of, but a person who became ideal only in response to Simon. It wasn't a thing she could tell him if he didn't find it out for himself.

"Silly," he said, "don't look so sad."

"I can't help it," Nina said. "I don't even understand what love is."

Simon sat down beside her. "Don't ruin your good mood for them. You can't do anything." He kissed her. Simon had such a wonderful mouth, warm and gentle without being mushy. "You smell good." He tickled her ear with his whisper.

They sat a moment cuddled together, and she knew she was happy with him. "Now," he said, "let's go back to the house, get something to eat along the way, maybe play some pool before dinner. Okay?"

"Okay," Nina jumped up. "Oh, Simon, I'm so glad we're us."

"Instead of Paul and Kim?"

"Instead of anyone."

But that night as they sat at dinner around the long fraternity dining table, all paired off with their dates, exchanging those terrible questions Nina had once hated so much (Where do you live, what's your major, how do you like college, do you think there is such a thing as a Mount Holyoke girl?), she felt a tiny nudge of dissatisfaction re-

164

new itself inside her. She and Simon would be silent at this dinner unless she made the effort of conversation. They would talk much more on Sunday, after the dates had gone; then she and Simon and his friends would review the weekend's high points, including a critique of the other girls. But tonight they took no part in this superficial talk; they had never taken part in it. Even when they first met, through friends at a party, they had been thoroughly sick of the dating atmosphere. But somehow, tonight, Nina wanted to discuss, to explain to someone in words what she was like, to have him think her fascinating.

Nina caught the eye of Tom, another of Simon's friends. He winked. "What's wrong?" he asked softly. "You look depressed." There it was: No one recognized her thinking, wishing look anymore. She was a petite, vivacious, feminine blonde, and somehow, perhaps because she curled the ends of her hair, she was deserving of an arm around the shoulder every now and then. But if there was ever a serious conversation, she was expected to have nothing to say.

It was different for Kim, who wore her beautiful red hair rebel-straight and her "artistic-cultured" flair loudly. She was the kind of girl whose presence compelled the boys to apologize if they happened to swear in front of her (Nina was glad they felt more relaxed with *her*, would never even think of an apology in her case). But then they would ask Kim what she was studying or how she liked the play, as if an affected manner of speech entitled her to an opinion. Even Paul treated her that way, as if they'd just met.

Dinner seemed to last forever. The couples were talking over their plans for the evening. Simon was still thinking about his hourly, though he held Nina's hand under the table so she wouldn't feel left out.

Nina tried not to listen to anyone else's conversation, but as her mind remained suspended aimlessly, her attention was drawn by a new clarity in the noises below. Only one person was talking, and she recognized the voice as Kim's.

"It's supposed to be one of the most beautiful movies ever made," she was saying. "Of course, I thought his *Taming of the Shrew* was marvelous; I love Michael York."

"I've seen it twice," one of the dates said. "I was terribly disappointed when it didn't win Best Picture of the Year."

"I've seen it twice on the stage," Kim continued. "I'm interested to see how Juliet is interpreted. Last time I saw her she rolled around the balcony and giggled."

Nina tried to think how long she had been wanting to see *Romeo and Juliet.* Over a year, she supposed. If they ever did go to the movies, Simon would pick Bergman or the Marx brothers. She couldn't remember the last time she'd seen a movie in color. Simon laughed at her for her love of extravaganza musicals, suggesting that she go to a matinee. But she didn't like to go to the movies alone, and she had pushed *Romeo and Juliet* toward the horizon of someday-when-he's-in-a-good-mood-and-doesn't-have-too-much-work. But now Paul and Kim were going, to hold hands in the theater and pretend *they* were Romeo and Juliet.

Why should they deserve to, why couldn't she and Simon go? She could ask. . . . No, she couldn't because she'd promised he could study.

Simon was looking her her. "What's wrong?" he whispered. "Want to leave?"

"Nothing." Nina always expected him to know what was wrong, and, besides, it was too painful to talk about immediately, in answer to a question.

"Come on, Nin," he said, "I know it's something. You have that certain look in your eyes." He brushed her hair off her forehead.

She tried to smile but failed miserably and had to blink to keep from falling over the brink of tears. Simon caught her hand and led her out of the room.

"Now you know we can't possibly get this straightened out unless you tell me what it is." He was worried.

"I know — you're right — I'm sorry; it's silly to get so upset — but, Simon, I want to do something."

"What?" he asked, surprised.

"Oh, I don't know — just not nothing — I'm so tired of doing nothing."

"Is that all? I thought it would be something terrible."

"It is terrible to me."

Simon was ruefully amused. "I knew this would happen when I saw you in that mood this afternoon. I knew you wouldn't want to study tonight."

"Please, please, can't we go somewhere?"

"Well, if you really want to, but I have to study for the test, so it will mean giving up something else. There's the football game tomorrow, and then the party, and Sunday night you'll want me to drive

167

you back; you know you hate to go back on the bus alone."

Why did he have to be so logical? "I don't care," she said, trying to express why. "It's not that I don't want to do all those things, it's just that," she groped, "that they're not what I really want to do." After she had said it, she recognized it as the answer: "We never do what I want to do."

Simon recognized the truth in what she said too. "All right. Tonight we'll do whatever you want; tomorrow we'll decide about the rest."

"Oh, Simon, that's wonderful. Are you sure? What shall we do?"

"No. You have to pick, that's the agreement. Do you have something special in mind?"

"Well —" Nina hesitated. "Yes, but I don't know what you —"

"What is it?" he demanded.

She felt blushy. "Would you mind — Paul and Kim are going too — do you think we could see *Romeo and Juliet?*"

"I suppose so. Is that something you've been wanting to do?"

She was surprised that he hadn't known. "Oh, yes. It's not that I think you're my Romeo or anything," she added, in case he was nervous about seeing a love story.

"I don't know, I've sometimes imagined myself as a prince." That streak of vanity in him surprised her; she'd forgotten about it because he was usually so sensible. She loved it for it made her feel closer to him, more like him.

"You'll have to help me decide what to wear. You look so pretty in that pink dress I don't want people to think we got together by accident. Should I wear a vest?"

"With jeans? I think you should wear your jeans, they make you look the handsomest. Whenever I went to mixers, the most beautiful boys would always wear jeans and wool jackets, but I never thought I could ever date one of them."

Finally they decided on the jeans, a sweater she had given him for his birthday, and a tweed jacket. Then Simon brushed the back of her hair for her as she watched his concerned look over her own head in the mirror in front of them. They met Paul and Kim and started for the theater.

"I'm sorry I got upset," Nina said.

"Don't be silly. You should tell me these things instead of keeping them all to yourself. I forget how things must seem to you."

"I know. I hate to end up making a scene."

"That's all right. . . . Besides, I sort of like it when you cry."

"Why?"

"It makes me feel strong when I can make you happy again."

"Oh, Simon, you're so silly," Nina said, but it was really an endearment.

At the theater they all sat up front so Nina wouldn't have to look over tall people's heads. The blank time before the movie started was awkward for all of them. Nina was beginning to feel guilty for bringing Simon away from his studying; he was depressed because he didn't take her out more and said horrible things he didn't mean, like, "Maybe you should go out with other people, and only come here every other weekend." Kim and Paul fought because Kim didn't want to go to another football game, and Paul had been particularly looking forward to the one the next day. They were all relieved when the lights went down.

During the beginning of the movie, Nina kept glancing at Simon to make sure he liked it. She needn't have worried.

"Look at the costumes," he whispered. "You'd like to live in a place like that, wouldn't you?" She was surprised he knew that about her; she'd thought he never guessed those things.

But soon the time for talk and extraneous thoughts was over as they were swallowed up by the story. Nina was in tears easily, from the time Romeo and Juliet parted at daybreak and Juliet wondered if she would ever see him again. How could two people be so young and beautiful and happy and really in love, and then die? Two lovers who had what everyone else tried for so hard — even poetry. Nina cried partly for her little love for Simon and how she would feel if she lost him; but mostly she cried for more than that, because she didn't know the depth of their love, because it was so terrible to be really in love, and she wasn't.

As the lights glared up too brightly, she looked at Simon and saw that he'd been crying too. And she didn't know enough about him to know why. But she would have liked to. They smiled at each other and kept silent.

Outside they walked behind Paul and Kim, who talked nonstop about the actors, the music, the direction.

Nina bubbled into a loud laugh. Simon looked down.

"I'm happy," she said.

"So am I. We should go out more often." .

"Oh, Simon, do you mean it?"

"Ummm. I was thinking, next term I don't want to be so bogged down in my work. We should go out and do different kinds of things. I don't want to spend my whole life learning — but then, when I think how little I know, my whole life could hardly begin —"

"You know, Simon, I forget how much I like you sometimes. I mean, I forget about parts of the way you are. I think, Simon's always this way, when you're not at all. . . . If I said I loved you a little, would it make you scared?" she asked bravely, on the spur of the moment.

He looked surprised, not as she'd thought he'd be, about love, but at the thought that he would mind.

"No, of course not, I'd be flattered — it would make me happy."

But, she thought, it wouldn't force him into saying the same thing. Not yet anyway, maybe never. But she'd found out long ago it was silly to play equals about love.

Nina slipped her head under Simon's arm and nestled there, where she could feel she belonged, for now.

THE GIRL WHO TALKED TO FROGS

THOMALINE AGUALLO BUCHAN

Charlotte is and always will be the girl who talks to frogs. Then, one golden day, Buddy comes along. . . .

The first thing Charley Moffit heard when she got to school in the morning was that Buddy Griffin was back in town.

"Oh, BOY!" she yelled, and did two leaps and a pirouette into American History II. She didn't care that girls in the hallway giggled quietly behind their hands and the boys just laughed out loud. Charley was used to knowing little smiles following her wherever she went. She knew all the kids thought her sort of weird.

"Why don't they like me?" she asked her friend Sue once, truly bewildered by the lack of an invitation to yet another party.

"Well, they *do* like you Charl, really, they do," said Sue, absently twisting a silken piece of the

172

hair that fell like thick coppery rain around her shoulders.

"Then why doesn't anyone ever ask me to go to the movies with them?" Charley persisted stubbornly, "or to join their club? Why didn't Sandy Tichenor ask me to her slumber party?"

"Oh, well," said Sue, twisting her small slim shoulders in agitation. She didn't like to hurt people, and she sensed that whatever she might say to Charlotte Moffit, sprawled dejectedly before her, the toes of her scuffed blue tennis shoes turned inward and drooping like a lost, sad child, would necessarily be wrong. "Well," said Sue again uncomfortably, "see, Charley, it's only . . . just . . . that the things you do are sort of different from the ones normal — that is, *most* kids like to do. At our age." Sue sat back, pleased with herself. There. That hadn't been *too* bad.

But Charlotte would not let it go at that. She never did; when subjects required pursuing she dogged them relentlessly to the bitter end. Grimly, and bit by bitter bit, she extracted from the unwilling Sue exactly what her schoolmates thought of her: She was wild and sloppy and clumsy and large. She liked to climb the low-hanging cliffs overlooking the ocean and look for lizards in the cracks when all the other girls were sampling lipsticks and eyelashes in the drugstore. She performed mysterious and smelly experiments in the basement of her grandfather's house while they shrieked wildly over JoJo Wickham's blue, blue eyes or Ricky Vega's wavy hair. They were 14 years old and standing, tense and expectant, on the threshold of Glorious Womanhood; she was 14 and an over-grown child; they sparkled and glowed with delicious femininity. She was, and would always be, the girl who talked to frogs. Then Buddy came along one golden Saturday and saved her.

Charley hurried as fast as her great big feet would carry her. It was the first Saturday in the month and Mr. Gansky would be putting something new in the front window of his pet store. She deliberately never asked what it would be, preferring to be surprised by whatever scaly treasure he chose to deposit there. Equally scrupulous, he never told her, on the other days she was in, what was coming. Gansky himself preferred it that way, liking to see the look of awe and delight on her fresh, pretty face, so clean and unspoiled. Not like those others, Gansky thought darkly, with the junk smeared three inches deep on their faces.

Charley almost ran the last half block to the pet store, then stopped abruptly a few feet from the door. Someone was already there, planted firmly in front of the window in her place. In *her place*. Rage built slowly and darkly deep within her battered navy pea coat. It was ruined now, her wonderful Saturday surprise, by some stupid *boy*. (She guessed it was a boy from the dark hair just brushing the neck of his sheepskin jacket and the heavy army boots sticking out beneath his jeans. Besides, hadn't everyone, from her mother on down, told her that no other girl in the world would spend a minute, let alone hours, staring at a bunch of smelly snakes?)

Dejectedly, she turned to go. She could never bear to share her happiness at the things she really loved, at any rate not since the age of nine, when she'd given her mother her favorite frog all wrapped up in a fancy box for her birthday. She could hear the shrieks now. Then, *"No. No,"* she thought determinedly. Not this time. There were few things in the world that meant anything to Charlotte Moffit, age 14, an outcast, but this was one of them. She turned again and marched regally, in ragged denim splendor, to the front of the store. Perhaps if she ignored him he would go away, and who cared anyway?

She cupped her hands against the glass to shade her eyes. She hoped it would be a monitor lizard, or maybe an iguana. An iguana! Wouldn't that be neat? She loved them; they looked like low-slung dinosaurs. She peered anxiously at a large fly walking over a pile of brown leaves in the corner of the window. Last week's mongoose was gone, and only these leaves were in evidence. The fly walked past one of the leaves, intent on a piece of chicken neck missed by the mongoose. The leaf opened its mouth, flicked out its tongue, and swallowed. The fly never knew what hit it.

"Oh!" Charley cried, and felt the boy turn expectantly toward her, waiting, she knew, for the inevitable girlish shriek of disgust and an accompanying grimace. Summoning her courage, she faced him squarely on her own grounds. "Some leaf!" she said, pointing her thumb at the Amazon tree frog.

"It's an Amazon," he said, approval shining at her through his thick, black-rimmed glasses. They were too big, and every few minutes he had to thumb them snugly back up the bridge of his bony nose.

175

"I know," she said importantly. "I used to have one when I was younger, but he ran away. At least that's what my mother said. I think maybe she just flushed him down the toilet. I used to talk to him down there, until one night she caught me." She stopped talking suddenly and felt her face go red with an unaccustomed blush.

"That's too bad," the boy encouraged, and shifted the pile of books he cradled in one arm to the other. He seemed to be waiting for her to go on.

Things spun madly in Charlotte Moffit's brain. No one in her life had ever cared to hear about the things she really loved. They told her to eat more string beans and inquired about her health. They remarked on her English marks and pointed out that her shoelaces were hanging by a thread. Her classmates borrowed her homework shamelessly and made fun of her behind her back. Only Sue cared anything about her at all, and *she* fainted at the thought of a mouse, let alone training a cageful of white ones. She was doomed, Charlotte told herself time and again, as she watched her parents melt slowly into the furniture and Sue pull away on the wave of her own beauty, to a life of simple loneliness.

"I guess you felt pretty rotten," the boy said, sitting down suddenly on the sidewalk and settling his back comfortably against the store wall. "I know just how you felt. The same thing happened to me and Disraeli."

Charley regarded him. He had stacked his books in neat little piles around him, suggesting a fortress, and seemed as settled as if he were in his own living room, and not sitting on a gum-sticky and littered sidewalk. "Have an Oreo," he said, reaching into the mysterious folds of an enormous canvas sack. He pulled a tired-looking cellophane package of cookies from his bag. "Or maybe an Oreo *crumb* is a better description," he said, regarding the tattered package critically.

"Or wait," he said, pulling at Charley's leg suddenly and bringing her down to his level with a *plop*. "How about an apple? Or some walnuts? I got plenty of walnuts, or wait, I think there might be an old Hershey bar down here. . . ." Frantically he rummaged through the bag. Charley saw flashes of things, like a glimpse of hidden treasure — a magnifying glass, a palette knife, some bird feathers tied neatly with a piece of twine, and what looked to be three baby diapers at the bottom of the pack. "Is Disraeli in there too?" said Charley, too fascinated to remember that she, whose only male speaking acquaintances at the moment were her father and Mr. Gansky, was speaking to a boy.

"Here," he said, handing her a notebook, magnet, some stick matches, and a flare, "No, Disraeli is gone. He was a snake, a king snake, a real beauty."

"Oh!" said Charley, "A king! How super!" She held the objects unquestioningly. They did, after all, belong to someone who had owned a king snake!

"Here it is!" said the boy triumphantly. He withdrew a large yellow banana and presented it to Charley with a flourish.

"But Disraeli," said Charley, peeling the banana dreamily.

"He was fantastic," said the boy. "About two feet long with thick creamy yellow stripes and dark, dark brown ones. And so nice, and really gentle, you know? I used to wear him on my arm and I swear he smiled at me."

"But what *happened?*" Charley prompted, giving an impatient little bounce on the cold, hard sidewalk.

"Oh, nothing really dramatic. I used to keep him in a box in my closet and he got in the habit of crawling into the pocket of a jacket that sometimes was on the floor." Charley, whose sweaters and jeans sometimes formed small, uneven mountains on *her* floor, found this reasonable. "So one day while I was at school, my ma decided to house clean and she sacked my room and gave away a whole bunch of my stuff to the Salvation Army. Including the jacket, and Disraeli, I guess, 'cause when I came home he was gone and I never found him."

"Oh," said Charley, aghast; and she placed a trembling hand on the front of her sweatshirt. Never, never, she thought, had she heard such a touching, *tragic* story. "I think . . . that's . . . just . . . OH!"

"I know," said the boy solemnly. "I feel the same about your tree frog."

"Listen," said Charlotte suddenly, a rush of pity overcoming her for this poor beleaguered soul, because what, after all, was a puny tree frog down the toilet compared to a kidnapped king? "Listen, this store, it's really super. Mr. Gansky has all kinds of frogs and things inside, in tanks and aquariums, and a bunch of lizards and monkeys, and a *koala bear*. He and I are personal friends," she said importantly. "It's sort of smelly, though. But I bet if you want, I can get him to let us in the back where he unpacks the wallabies!" He smiled a chocolate cookie smile.

After that Charlotte often wondered how she'd gotten through life without a real friend. There was Sue, of course, her friend from sandbox days. Although Sue really liked her, weren't they more friends because their mothers were? Now Sue was in the throes of discovering who she was, and spent long minutes staring in the mirror at her small, piquant face, and touching her long shining hair in almost-caresses. Charlotte could only stare at her and listen to Sue and her girl friends laughing their sly, secret giggles in the hall; there was a secret they knew which she did not. It had something to do with being a woman. Sue could not tell her and her mother would not. Perhaps they knew, as she suspected deep in herself, she was not worthy to know. She wouldn't really care about it, thought Charlotte, on another long, gray afternoon of walking by herself, if only she were not so lonely. Everywhere she looked she saw units of people talking and touching and laughing, as though they really cared what the other ones thought. She would drag her heels a little harder and pull her jacket collar forward as if to hide, and wish she were a boy, or dead, or both. Then one day it seemed someone must have said, "There, *that* one, give her something, the poor droop; no one should be *that* unhappy." And she got Buddy.

Noel Griffin called himself Buddy and didn't care who liked it. "My mother reads a lot of mushy novels," was all he would say about his name. He himself chose Buddy after giving Winston, Tiger, and Captain Zoom a whirl. He was 15½ years old and precocious. The wall of books he built around himself and Charlotte Moffit the day they met included *The Notebooks of Leonardo da Vinci, 1001 Experiments with Insects, African Genesis*, a Judy Collins songbook, and two very battered books of Hardy Boys stories he'd found on his weekly prowl of secondhand bookstores.

He did not think himself odd for preferring the company of fossils and rocks and sea cliffs to that of other humans. Most of his classmates were older than he and regarded him as a very amiable but slightly lunatic pet. He was their bright boy; he won debates for them and wrote stirring editorials for the school newspaper naming names about which teachers always hogged the student parking lot, and said that most of the 18 year olds he knew would rather get the vote than get stoned. They liked him from eight till three, then promptly forgot about him. He didn't mind. "The guys just care about their cars," he told Charlotte, "and girls. And the girls — well," he said almost wistfully, "they look nice and they smell good. But there's no use kidding myself. I won't be ready for them for at least five years, and they might *never* be ready for me."

Charley agreed. She agreed with everything Buddy said. Both of them reeled at the thought of the other. They were perfect together. They would sit on the sidewalk outside Gansky's place for hours sometimes, waiting for the familiar red-and-white panel truck to come from the air freight terminal at L.A. International. Who knew what it might carry? An assortment of monkeys from South America, wallabies from Australia, and startled-looking otters from Europe. Mr. Gansky never told them when he was going to the airport to pick up a new shipment, but more often than not, as he drew near the store he would see up ahead those two — those crazy *kids* again — sitting on the sidewalk, chins in hand, looking past the highway traffic right at his truck, right *through* the truck he often thought, at the cargo of tree snakes and freshwater tropical fish. They always had their leather gloves to handle the nervous fox kits and skittish ocelot babies. They never once asked his permission; they just seemed to know he wouldn't mind being helped. They never asked for pay and only wanted to be told the habits and habitats of the creatures instead.

On the other weekends they would go to the tidepools along the shore, giggling over the Charlie Chaplin hermit crabs scuttling along the rocks, and they would climb the bluffs on the beach and stalk the prickly horned toads that were so very gentle in their hands despite their fierce looks. He showed her how to catch the faster alligator lizards for which Gansky paid them 20¢ each. They never sold a horned toad, but the alligator lizards furnished quite a few malts and an occasional hot dog at the pier, where they would also lie flat on the ground and look at clouds, and take crazy pictures in the five-for-a-quarter machine.

They hunted lizards in single file, in what they called their caveman fashion, scouring the ground with narrowed eyes to detect the slightest flicker of tiny legs or a dry rustle in the tough, dead grass. If they froze quickly enough after first seeing the lizard, it usually stopped to look around. Then it

181

was easy to slip a tiny noose (made from the kite strings in which the California hillsides seemed to spin themselves every April) over the lizard's faceted head. Then, with a delicate upward tug of the kite string "fishing pole," Buddy would lift it off the ground and into a shoebox. Only he could pull that one off. Charley's hands felt like boxing gloves when she tried it once, and thereafter she resigned herself to merely mouthing oohs and aahs.

On Charley's fifteenth birthday she got a wonderful present and a shock. She had two birthdays, really. Her birthday, commemorating the date she was born, when her parents gave her an electric toothbrush, a hamper for her dirty clothes, some underwear, and the news that her semiannual dental appointment would be next week, was on a Friday.

On Saturday her *real* birthday with Buddy began. After months of pleading, he had finally consented to take her all-day fishing with him on the breakwater. "You really wouldn't like it, Charley," he'd said dubiously. "It gets very wet and cold. It's winter, don't forget, and I stay until dark."

"I don't care!" she would cry; it was the only thing he had refused her, and sometimes he wavered — there was that picture in his mind of poor Charlotte being washed over by a wave in the dark, but finally he consented, for her birthday, to take her along. They packed a basketful of all the things they liked: thick slabs of ham and cheese and a package of still-warm homemade tortillas from the Mexican deli; big chunks of dark chocolate-colored honeycomb; bottles of frosty root beer, and a thermos of steaming cocoa.

182

Buddy packed the fishing equipment. Charley carried the straw picnic basket under one arm and her birthday gift from Buddy under the other; no one had ever told her it was possible to be so happy. The laughter bubbled to the top of her throat like popcorn popping and sometimes just spilled out. It would have been enough, she thought, just to be with him on this crisp, apple-fresh day, tramping along side by side, but no, he had given her a wonderful, magic book too, called *The Glass Harmonica*. The pages were thick and filled with wonderful words about witches and goblins and fairies. "How did you know?" she wanted to say, loving it so; but, then, how could he not? He knew her so well. She sometimes thought he must know places inside her even she was afraid to see. How was she to know it was to be their last good day together?

They were on their way back, picking their way carefully over the fog-slicked stone blocks, each the size of a sedan. Slung over his shoulder he carried the dripping, clackery gunnysack of crabs, while she brought up the rear with the picnic basket and a plastic bucket of buttermouth perch. The fog was getting thick and Charley kept her eyes glued to the back of Buddy's jacket.

Then a voice came out of the gray blank air. "If you boys are goin' back in, how 'bout lettin' us have your bait?" The voice's owner appeared — a huge man dressed in a fur-lined parka. His partner, as small as the other was large, wore an army fatigue jacket and a carpet. They had a good fire of driftwood and briquets going. True to breakwater custom, Buddy handed over their box of shrimp bait and they were promptly invited for a bit of the sand bass dinner being cooked by the men over a 1934 radiator grill stuck in a rock niche. Charley stuffed eight sand bass into her mouth and felt their heat settle comfortably into her belly. Blissfully she gulped the ashen-tasting black coffee they gave her.

"Sorry we called the girl friend a boy," the big man said.

"Oh, that's okay," said Buddy pleasantly. "She doesn't care. She practically *is* a boy." Charlotte basked in the warmth of his praise.

"Me an' my sister," the small man said, "we used to be pretty close. Usta fish together; even do a little huntin'."

"We mostly climb a lot," said Buddy, "and stuff like that." He stopped and stared at Charley. "Boy," he said slowly, "You know? I'm really going to miss all this when I go."

Charlotte put her soup can of coffee down. "Go?" she said, not understanding. "But where? Why do you have to go?"

"To *college*, dummy," said Buddy fondly. "I graduate at the end of the month, remember?"

Dimly Charley pulled from her mind the fact that Buddy was older than she; not only that, he had skipped grades. More than that was the knowledge that though the time they spent together seemed like one long day, months, in fact, had slipped past since they first met. The others were talking now, and laughing, of fish they'd caught or let get away. Charlotte pressed the warm can of coffee to her cheek. A coldness was beginning in her which not the coffee or all the blankets in the world could make go away. . . .

There was a strange car in the Moffit driveway as Charley rounded the corner on the run. She had known there would be. It was the Griffins' of course; Buddy's mother or father had brought him. It didn't matter now that he had left her to flounder helplessly like a beached fish without him. It didn't matter that she had returned to her solitary way of life with only his letters to keep her going. It didn't even matter that, though she wrote him volumes (and sent him clippings she thought he would like, and tiny paper-thin shells with the sand baked on them to make him think of home), he sent only breathless short notes back and then, finally, the last few months, nothing. Nothing mattered now that he was back.

"Buddy!" she cried, crashing through the laundry room and into a pile of her mother's freshly washed sheets.

"Oh, Charlotte," Mrs. Moffit said, "Why can't you learn to watch where you're going? Here," she said, disentangling her daughter from the twisted, wet sheets, "don't move an *inch*. I might be able to keep them off the floor."

"But *Buddy!*" Charley said pleadingly.

"Well, Buddy came specifically to see you, and he's only been here for 20 minutes. I think he'll wait five more."

"Where is he?" said Charley impatiently. "In my room? Did you tell him I had three new frogs?"

"No," said Mrs. Moffit, expertly pulling the last sheet from under Charlotte's elbow. "I left that exciting news to you. He's in the living room talking to Daddy, as a matter of fact." That seemed odd. Buddy had never much cared for grown-up conversation, limited as it was, he said, to What Did You Learn in School Today?

The door pushed open and her father appeared, with Buddy right behind him. At least she supposed it was Buddy. Those were Buddy's eyes, anyway: laughing and dark and glowing. But the rest of him was very — different from the Buddy who had gone. This Buddy was taller and slightly heavier. The hollows in his chest and belly and around his spindly legs had all filled out. He wore his brown corduroy pants and beige cable-knit, turtleneck sweater with a solid, easy grace. Buddy! Who never cared what, or if, he wore anything at all! She stared, open-mouthed in wonder. "You're so . . . beautiful!" she said.

Her parents laughed. "Beautiful!" her mother said. "Oh, Charlotte. Men aren't beautiful, they're *handsome*. I must admit, though, Noel, you've really filled out nicely."

"Noel!" said Charley loudly.

He looked sheepish for a minute, and almost like his old, real self. "Well, I asked your folks to call me that, Charl," he said. "Everyone at school does."

An awkward silence settled, then, "Your glasses," Charley said finally, "you don't wear your glasses anymore either."

"Well, no," he admitted, "I got contact lenses. Everybody told me I would look better."

"And you do," Mrs. Moffit agreed. "Don't you think so, Charlotte?"

"I think he just got tired of dropping his glasses in his soup all the time," she said unkindly.

"Charlotte!" her father said.

Buddy laughed and shook his head. "She's still the same, isn't she?" he said over her head to her father. Charley drew back in quiet horror. He was talking to her in *that way:* as if she almost weren't there, and in a terrible kind of patronizing tone he used to say adults used with dogs and dim-witted children.

"Do you still like to hunt for lizards?" he asked politely.

"Sometimes," said Charley, coolly but equally polite. "Do you?"

"Oh, no," he said, "I don't really have time for anything but the books. I made some new friends and we sort of, you know, help each other along." He turned to the senior Moffits. "I'm trying to get into Scripps, you know," he said. "I'd like to be an oceanographer." That was better, Charley thought. There was a little of Buddy left in Noel Griffin, after all.

"Well," he said at last, "I guess I'd better move. I have to be in L.A. at five and I'm not sure my car will make it. It knocks." His own car, she thought.

"Have you checked your spark plugs?" asked Mr. Moffit.

"No," said Buddy, interested at once. "Say, do you think that might be it?"

"Let's have a look," said Charlotte's father.

"That would be great," said Buddy, starting out the door. "Oh," he said, turning directly to her for the first time. "Wait. Charley, I almost forgot. I brought you something."

He reached underneath his sweater and withdrew a chubby, brightly colored stuffed frog with poppy

187

eyes. "I thought you might like this," he said shyly, pushing it into her limp palm. "A friend of mine helped me pick it out — I told her, make it something for a really nice kid who's nuts about creepy crawlers."

A *kid!* Charley touched the frog's button eyes. It had scaly-looking hair and a silly, vacuous expression just, she thought, like her own. It was something you would give a kid, a child.

Well, she thought, watching her father and Buddy — no, *Noel* — peering intently under the hood of his car, *why not?* That's what she'd been when he left. A year had been nothing to her; it might have been a minute. Yet for him, another world had opened up and he had left her behind. But hadn't he given her more than just a toy, or a book, or a few happy days? He had given her himself when she needed something stronger to hold onto, and most of all he'd given her a sense of herself, a feeling of pride in who she was and who she would become.

Suddenly she did not hate the Buddy who had come back to her, or the life he lived without her. Time had passed and he was almost a man. Time would pass for her too someday, and in the same way; she would be a woman. Until then, well, there was always time.

MY GRANDPA'S LUMP OF FIVE
WASTED YEARS

WILLIAM VINCENT BURGESS

*Georgina thinks that digging for gold is the best
way to spend a summer. She is too young to know
that she might find something even more important
— love.*

When I was a pig-tailed tomboy I spent each summer with my grandparents Haskin. They lived in
the next state, in Idaho, in a big brown house that
I remember most for its curtains. All the front
windows were awash with lace, and this lace was
patterned with ears of corn and squirrels and wide-
winged eagles and all kinds of flowers. I used to
trace my fingers along these shapes, and sometimes
I made up stories about them. And once I dreamed
it was snowing, and the snow was white lace curtains embroidered by Grandmother Haskin.

But if these front curtains made me think of

winter, the kitchen curtains, sour-green gingham tied back with red and yellow ribbons, reminded me of spring and apple blossoms; and the curtains in Grandpa's study were long, shaggy, bear-brown memories of fall. They were my most favorite curtains, and they were in my most favorite place.

Looking back, I suppose that a part of what made it my most favorite place was that I wasn't ever supposed to be in that room on my own. It was Grandpa's room; no one else used it, though the door was never locked. I used to sneak in, whenever I could, just to look at the place on the mantelpiece where the five wasted years had been.

I was six when I first found out about the five years, and I can still recall the excitement of the discovery. Of course, I'd seen it the year before, and the year before that, I suppose, but I hadn't known about it. It was just a slab of what looked like ordinary gray rock, except that some of it was gold and twinkled when you moved your head.

On this day, however, I was Grandpa's guest in his study, and I felt I had to talk to him. So I asked him what it was. He looked at it for awhile and then he looked back at me. Then he got up and lifted it from the mantelpiece and put it on the table.

"That, Miss Georgina," he said, "is five wasted years of my life. Five wasted years, that's what that is."

I looked at it. I had never seen five years before. "Is it real?" I asked.

"Five wasted years," he repeated. Then he said, "Course that was afore I met your grandma, y'understand?"

"Can I touch it?" I whispered.

"Go right ahead, ma'am," he said, stepping back from the table.

I put out my hand and held my breath. With my other hand I kept hold of Grandpa's arm. I think I expected to be burned or stung. I know I was expecting something to happen, and I was surprised when nothing did. The five wasted years was cold and rough and so heavy I couldn't lift it. The little pieces of gold glittered back at me when I touched them.

"Are all them glitterin' parts the months in the five years?" I asked him.

"Miss Georgina," he said, "you're a smart one — how come you guessed that so quick?"

I felt very proud about this, and so I said, "Oh, I jus' sorta knew all along, I guess."

As he was putting it back on the mantelpiece I said, "I never knew you could have a lump of five years. Does everyone have five years in a lump like that?" I was wondering what had happened to mine.

"Well, no — like I said, that lump there *is* wasted years, and not all folks waste time. All folks ain't that foolish. Your grandma now, I don't reckon she'd have a lump of five wasted minutes — or your mamma."

"What about me?"

"I can't rightly see as you've had all that much time to waste, can you?"

"No." I said, "I'm only six."

That night, as I lay in bed, I thought it all over, and when I heard Grandpa climbing the stairs I called out to him. When he was sitting on the edge of my bed I asked him, "If you can waste time, an' it's for sure good an' proper waste, how'd you get it in a lump like that'n down in your study?"

"Well, I guess it just depends on how you waste it," he said.

"How did you waste it?" I asked.

"Diggin' for gold," he said.

I sat up at once. This was better than I had imagined. "Diggin' for gold!" I shouted. "Did you do that? Did you find any? What did you do with it?"

"Now, there ain't no need to get yourself so uncovered," he said, fussing with the bedclothes. "I only found fool's gold."

"What's that?"

"Well, miss, let me tell you 'bout that. Fool's gold sure looks like gold an' sure feels like gold an' I'll wager if'n it could smell it'd stink like gold, but it sure an' for certain ain't gold. It's the devil's imitation. It's just a waste of time."

"Like your five years' lump, you mean?"

"Jus' like those five wasted years."

And, of course, that did it. For the remainder of that long, happy-as-a-birthday summer I dug for gold. I even managed to persuade my friend Timber Woods to help me. Timber Woods was five and bright. It didn't seem to matter that he was a boy; he was my best friend.

We sat down on his back porch and figured things out. If we found gold, we'd be rich. I was going to buy a real-life railway engine, and Timber was going to be the President of the United States so that he could make every day be Christmas Eve. And we were going to get our folks everything they wanted.

And if we didn't find any gold, we had it figured

that that meant a waste of time. And two whole months of wasted time each meant quite a big lump for Timber and me; or maybe (we hadn't quite sorted this part of things out) we'd have just one large lump of four months between us. We didn't much mind which way it turned out; either way we couldn't lose. Mind you, we weren't too certain where the lump of wasted time was going to come from, but I was positive we'd get it. And after I'd managed to sneak Timber into Grandpa's study to see the five years, he was positive too.

After a few weeks, when the back garden was pitted with holes, Grandma said we were worse than a pair of gophers, and she shooed us off to dig elsewhere. We had a word with Grandpa then. We never mentioned the waste-of-time part; we just told him we were searching for gold. As one old-timer to another, he suggested the old over-grown field behind the house. "Seems like I ain't ever noticed afore how rich that soil is," he said. "Reckon I might start in diggin' there along with you."

And he did too! All that summer we were out there digging — Grandpa, Timber, and me. Day after day after dusty day — or so it seemed then. Actually, I remember how that was the year Timber and I learned to swim. And there was a trip to the mountains and a visit to the fair in old St. Paul. And on Sundays none of us did anything, for that was the Sabbath and we were God-fearing. But all the rest of the time we just dug like prairie dogs in November.

The week before I was due to go home I had another talk with Grandpa. This time, though, I

193

had Timber with me. We came straight to the point.

"D'you think we're goin' to find any gold?"

"Well now, let me think 'bout that." Grandpa closed his eyes and leaned back into his chair. Timber stared up at the five years; I pretended that I was used to seeing it.

"After due consideration" — Grandpa opened his eyes again — "I don't reckon there's been much gold found 'round hereabouts. Not that I can recall here anyways."

"Well, Grandpa, that's what we figured too. And Timber 'n' me, we reckon that as we didn't find anythin', we sure are entitled to a good hunk of wasted time each, and how do we go 'bout gettin' it?"

Grandpa stood up and placed one hand on the five wasted years. "Georgina, Timber boy, you know, sometimes I get forgetful. I ain't so young no more. I jus' can't remember where exactly I did get my lump of five years. Maybe we ain't dug sufficient. You thought on that?"

We shook our heads.

"An' maybe they don't do no lumps of under five years' size, you ever think on that?"

We shook our heads again.

"Five years is all I am, Mr. Haskin," said Timber sadly.

"I know, boy, I know," said Grandpa, just as sadly. "Tell you what. I got a hunch that if we dug 'round that old withered pecan tree, the one near the top of the field, I reckon we might find us a thing or two. Mind you, it's just a hunch — I ain't certain — nothin' mightn' happen."

The next day was full of thrills. In the early part

of the afternoon when we were all digging away by the pecan tree Timber found an Indian arrowhead, and he showed it to Grandpa.

"Well, I'll be a long-eared mule!" shouted Grandpa. "That there's a Sioux arrowhead! They're mighty rare 'round these parts. That's the real thing, you know, boy. Genuine Sioux! Give you a dollar for it?"

Timber shook his head, his eyes wide.

"Make it two dollars then!" Grandpa shouted eagerly.

"No, sir," said Timber. His voice was breathless, but determined.

"Where 'bouts d'you find it?" I asked him.

He pointed to the ground at his feet. It was the only part of the field that we hadn't dug over and there were weeds with red flowers growing there and sharp, stinging grass. Here and there were bare patches of soil where, Grandpa said, old Mrs. Mahoney's dog had buried his bones.

I began to dig. Then Grandpa began to dig. Then Timber started again. By suppertime we had found 20 arrowheads. We wanted to carry on, but Grandpa said it wouldn't have been much use. Sioux Indians, he said, never buried more than 20 arrowheads at a time. We had been lucky to find the whole 20, he told us, most folks didn't find that many. Why, look at him, he said, he'd only found two. Timber and I had nine each. Grandpa went up to ten dollars each for those arrowheads, but we refused. They were like gold to us.

We left the field and entered the house, bursting with excitement and shouting for Grandma. But as we rushed into the kitchen she came out to meet us, looking straight at Grandpa. "Adam, it's happened! Like we always know'd it would. Your five wasted years is gone!"

Grandpa ran into his study, and Timber and I raced after him. On the mantelpiece was nothing. Grandpa sat down in his chair. Grandma said, "I've been expectin' this to happen."

"You're right," said Grandpa. "Wasted time just always goes in the end. You never have anythin' to show for it. But Indian arrowheads and well-dug fields, well, they last forever. And I got me one very well-dug field jus' ready for plantin', and you got eighteen of those genuine arrowheads, 'n' I reckon that's better 'n any old lump of wasted time."

"That's the truth," said Grandma, and Timber and I just nodded.

And that's all, really. When I came back the following year the five years still hadn't come back, and Timber had moved to another town. I never saw him again, but the five wasted years, well, I saw that last week. Grandpa sent it to me as a twenty-first birthday present. He'd had it carved into a paperweight, shaped like an arrowhead.

With it came a note. "Dear Georgina," it said. "This began as five wasted years. But now, as I send it to you, it is a long summer filled with laughter. Thank you. Adam Haskin."

A MEMORY OF BUTTERFLIES

THOMALINE AGUALLO

Lainie loves the world she sees. Then tragedy strikes and Lainie learns that loving the world means more than just loving beautiful beaches and warm earth.

This was to be the summer Lainie fell in love with things. She decided at its beginning that it would not be a summer of waste and regret. Now would be the time. She would walk through fresh new fields feeling the scratch of wild grass against her tanned, bare legs, feeling the wind whip her hair around her face, feeling the touch on her hand of the things other people called butterflies. (How could you give such an ordinary thing as a name to these wisps of woven tapestry floating in the air?) Lainie would lie in the warm grass and close her eyes, and they would alight on her. She would look at them, these rare bits of translucent loveliness, and how proud of them she would be — proud of their beauty and delicacy and grace, and proud of herself too, if it were known, to be the one to whom butterflies came.

Every morning Lainie would rise at six and watch the fiery golden drops of melting sun spread smoothly over the calm sea. She would throw open her bedroom window and breathe deeply, allowing great mouthfuls of tangy salt air to settle in her lungs. Then she would grin happily and hug herself, knowing that here was another day not lost. She was now free — free within herself and free, suddenly, from the parental restrictions that still bound many of her friends. Her mother was at her grandmother's house a hundred miles away. The voice that ordinarily spoke of orderly and constructive things to do ("Clean out your closets, wash your bedroom rug. . . .") was far away and silent. Lainie's father saw in her young and eager face only the signs he had carefully memorized when she was three and seven and nine. She was that girl to him, that little girl of quiet ways. He heard the slap of her tennis shoes on her bedroom floor and sat across from her at the kitchen table and still offered her colored ribbons for the pigtails she no longer wore. He did not know what was happening to her.

For Lainie was different this year — different from the T-shirted, chalk-knuckled child she had been last year. Different too from the girl who waited for her in her future. This year she was fourteen, and something was happening to her. One day she had known that someone else was coming alive inside her — someone she would not quite recognize. But as the days and months flew past her, the someone else took shape and form. She knew instinctively that next year it would be someone else who slipped her feet into Lainie's shoes, who made her bed and read her books; someone else would answer to Lainie's name. And so the Lainie who still was felt oddly and defiantly compelled to cling somehow to the childish and childlike dreams she knew so well. The woman she was already beginning to become stood waiting quietly in the shadows, while *she* raced madly through the summer days, her eyes searching and eager to see, her fingers ready to touch, her sense breathtakingly alive.

I will know things this year, she told herself. *I will taste them and touch and feel.* And she would race down the steps of her beach-front house with only two thin strips of cloth covering her body. She would throw herself into the warm sand, not caring if it got into her hair, and she would close her eyes and lift her face to the sun and feel its warmth seep slowly into her golden skin. *I am colors*, she would think lazily, allowing words to drift into place and never worrying whether or not they made sense. *I am rainbows and kaleidoscopes and prisms catching light. I am pieces of the sun falling through the trees, spilling over leaves onto the ground. I am the night in a silent velvet coat, I am colors. I am pieces of the sun. . . .*

The sound of these words pleased her, and she said them aloud, rolling them around her tongue. Sometimes she wrote them down, and it pleased her to see her words written in her firm hand on pink and orange paper, hidden carefully in her flowered notebook. She made friends with words this year and searched greedily for sensations that could be transferred to paper to keep them alive forever in her memory.

She was swept up in an aura of her own emotions. She sucked sweet flower stems and dug her hands into the soft, rich earth of her mother's garden. Some evenings she sat curled up in a chair and stared dramatically into the night. Her head held high, eyes misty with thought, she would let words come again. Across the room another human being who only coincidentally happened to be her father, and who did not know her dreams but vaguely remembered his own, watched her face and wished his wife were there to remember too.

And so Lainie's days melted away, one into another, and quietly the specter of fall and school and responsibility began to loom in her mind. She found, to her horror, that there were still many things she had to do, and time, time, time — where did it go and why did it elude her? She raced frantically through the days, gobbling up experiences and swallowing them whole. All of a sudden she began to feel a breathless, choking feeling in her heart when night would come and another day was gone.

Then one day she came home, opening the door noisily, trailing bits of sand over her mother's new wool rug. She did not sense anything wrong in the house at first, so busy was she sorting out the details of her day, selecting things she might tell her father, who enjoyed listening to her talk, and thinking of things she would write to her mother — things that would sound reasonable and constructive. She must reassure her mother that she had been right to leave her and her father alone. She was doing the dishes and hanging up her clothes, and there was no need for her mother to come home and seal off the little time she had left to herself.

The darkness of the house bewildered her. Usually her father was home by now, puttering around in the kitchen. But no lamp was lit, no music spilled from the hi-fi in the corner of the living room, and Lainie stood, suddenly alert, and tried to think of where her father could be. She did not know why she worried; her father was a careful man, and he often arrived home after her. She calmed herself by thinking about why he might be late.

There would be light for *him* when he came home, she thought righteously, and there was. And *Sergeant Pepper* was playing on the phonograph, and a good bacony smell filled the house. Lainie herself was singing lustily along with Ringo as she made her special apple and avocado salad.

He came into the kitchen, where she was, and he wondered how to tell her. She saw him and threw her arms around him and started to tell the story of the little boy and his kite. He tried to say "Lainie," and finally had to disentangle himself from her entirely to get a word in edgewise. "Lainie," he said quietly, and he tried to keep the fear out of his voice, "we've got to go out to Grandma's tonight."

"Tonight!" she cried. "But why? For how long? Is Mother coming home? I was going to the caves tomorrow. Look, I could stay with Sheila and you could go. . . ." Her mind raced ahead, and she saw the days restricted drastically by her mother's reappearance into her life. She loved her mother but resented this intrusion and what it would mean. She felt the hard pressure of her father's hands on her shoulders, and his words penetrated her self-pity. She realized then, that he was saying, "Your grandmother is dying, Lainie. Mother needs us. I don't know how long we'll be away. We may already be too late. Your grandmother is dying."

Silently she turned from him and went to pack her clothes.

It took Lainie a few minutes in the morning before she knew where she was. Her eyes rested sleepily on the unfamiliar room around her, and she wondered for a moment where the sea gulls were before she remembered the hurried packing and grim journey of the night before. She had dozed off a dozen times during the three-hour pilgrimage to her grandmother's house. Her grandmother lived one hundred miles inland, away from the ocean, in a hot, dusty area Lainie did not like. The house had been her mother's home. It had once been a small ranch, and Lainie vaguely remembered the horses and chickens and maybe a cow, but that had been when her grandfather was alive. When he died, Lainie's grandmother had tried vainly to hold onto the land, but it proved to be too much, and little by little it slipped away from her until all that was left was the house and a little land around it for a garden and her precious chickens. Lainie's parents had tried to persuade the old woman to live with them, but she was stubborn and wanted to stay where she was. So all through Lainie's life there were hot, tiring trips to dry, drab land (in Lainie's opinion) where the sun was an enemy, hot and dry and scorching. You could only stand it in the morning, because at night the temperature plummeted, and you couldn't go out. So for Lainie, the trips to Grandma's house were things to be borne, like crosses. And although she was, she supposed, fond of her grandmother and loved her as one loves one's relatives, still there was little fun in being told to play quietly because noises gave Grandma a headache, or to play outside so you wouldn't knock over any of the several thousand knick knacks her Grandma had teetering precariously on wooden shelves. There was no one around for Lainie to play with, and she would become bored and cranky and, inevitably, she would do something to annoy her grandmother, who would purse her wrinkled lips and make blunt observations about spoiled, modern children as though Lainie were not even there. Lainie, being a spoiled, modern child, would react verbally, her mother would cry out in vexation, and her father would submerge himself in a newspaper. Every day spent there seemed to end in tears and recriminations, with Lainie relegated to the back seat of the car on the trip home.

As she grew older, it was somehow tacitly agreed that everyone's mental health would benefit greatly if Lainie's presence at her grandmother's house were curtailed sharply. And there were times when her parents would set off for whole weekends without her — a dutiful note of love from Lainie to her grandmother tucked away in her mother's purse. When they returned, her mother would carry a similar note to Lainie, plus a plateful of oatmeal-raisin cookies. Lainie never knew why her grandmother thought she liked oatmeal-raisin cookies.

Lainie and her father had driven in silence all

the way to her grandmother's house. What her father's thoughts were, she did not know. And she cared less. The words *it isn't fair, it isn't fair* ran through her mind over and over, until they became a cadence of sorrow and she dwelt in them. It just *wasn't* fair, she thought, when the whole summer had been so good, and *she* had been so good. She had stepped carefully around ants, so conscious was she of living things, and she had fed a stray kitten, and rescued a sodden ladybug from the sea. All these things she had done with love. So how could this happen to someone who would spare little ants?

"It isn't fair," she cried out suddenly, and she was surprised as her father to hear the words escape from her mouth. But she plunged on recklessly. "Why should I have to go? I can't do anything for Grandma. I can't do anything yet for anyone but me! I'll only get in the way, and everyone will be even more unhappy."

They were almost there then. As they got closer, she saw the lights from her grandmother's house flickering forlornly in the distance, and finally her father pulled to a stop.

He looked at her with eyes of pain. "Haven't you any compassion, Lainie?" he asked. "Aren't you even sorry that your grandmother is dying?"

"Of course I am!" she said angrily. "But what good will it do? Is it going to make her any better? Besides," she went on stubbornly, "she's old. It's what you should expect when you're old." (Lainie would never grow old.)

Her father shook his head in exasperation. "The only thing I'm sorry about right now," he said, "is that you are my daughter."

Then they could say no more, for her mother had opened the door and stood waiting, framed by the dying firelight behind her. She looked tired and sad, and she hugged Lainie fiercely to her. "I'm so glad you're both here," she said. "I'm so glad."

Lainie stood woodenly, arms hanging at her side, as her mother's arms tightened around her. Without warning, tears began to slide down her face, and she turned her head into the warm, smoky roughness of her mother's robe trying to hide them. "Oh, Lainie, no," her mother said. "Don't cry, sweetheart. Grandma is still alive, but," her voice faltered slightly, "she's so very sick, I really don't know. Look, you go take a peek at Grandma. She's sleeping now, but it doesn't matter because she doesn't recognize people anymore. Take a peek and go to bed."

Lainie left her parents and tiptoed down the hall. She opened the door to her grandmother's room and looked at the old woman lying there, tossing fitfully in her sleep. "I am sorry, Grandma, truly I am," she whispered to the covered form. "But there is nothing I can do for you." Then the close, stale odor of sickness and age overwhelmed her. She closed the door.

Lainie tied the belt of her robe tight against her stomach. It was eleven o'clock when she finally awakened, and now it was almost noon. But the house was still. Too still, she thought suddenly, and she hurried to the kitchen, fearful that something had happened during the long night.

Her father sat drinking coffee at the table. He looked at her but said nothing, and Lainie, sitting down, became suddenly shy and remembered with a shock how she and her father had become almost strangers.

"Grandma —" she began.

"Sleeping," he said. "The doctor has just gone. She's fairly comfortable and doing as well as can be expected. But your mother is the one I'm worried about, Lainie. She's tired and she's scared. So if it isn't too much trouble, will you please try to present at least a facade of sympathy? I know you think she's too fussy and too hard on you sometimes, but if you could try to remember for awhile that she's not just your mother now, but someone's daughter." He looked at her carefully. And then, having made up his mind that his words were wasted, shrugged his shoulders and left.

Lainie sat at the kitchen table and watched her mother through a window. She stood, hands in the pockets of a dress Lainie knew well, and stared unseeing at the careful, neat rows of flowers around her. They stayed that way for awhile — her mother standing in the yard and Lainie watching from the kitchen. Then somehow Lainie was walking the few steps to her mother. *She's not just your mother now, but someone's daughter. . . .* Lainie's mind echoed with her father's words. She looked at her mother's small, straight back and wondered, for the first time, what it felt like to stand in the sun and know your mother was nearby, dying.

"I used to pick the flowers, you know," her mother said, almost to herself. *"We* used to, I mean. My mother and I. We'd come out here in the morning, and my mother would water her flowers and mix the earth, and I'd watch her work. Sometimes I would just lie on the grass and watch her and the butterflies. I loved to watch them fly and land." She smiled. "I have such memories right now, Lainie," she said, acknowledging her daughter's presence.

Lainie's mind looked to the past and saw her mother as a girl, a child, lying on the grass, looking wonderingly at the tiny, jeweled butterflies, as Lainie herself so often did. Then her mind raced ahead and projected itself into the future, and she was Lainie grown older, with children of her own, and waiting.

The sound of her mother's voice brought her back to the present. "I know how hard this is on you, darling," she was saying. "I know you don't want to be here — hot and lonely and waiting for death — but I was standing here remembering and I wondered what you would say, if I — if I were to tell you, Lainie, that I love you and I need you very much." Suddenly she was silent, standing awkwardly in front of her daughter. And all at once Lainie saw not the machine-mother who accomplished the care and feeding of her family and home in a cool, efficient manner, but a woman — a woman who was suffering and in need of help.

Lainie felt tears beginning to brim at her eyes, but she knew instinctively that the time was not yet right for tears. Tears were waiting for them all around the corner soon enough. Now was the time for comfort. So, smilingly, she answered her mother's question.

"I guess I would just say," she said softly, "that I love you too." Quietly she took her mother's hand, and together they walked out of the sun and into the old quiet house.

AFTER ALL, WE'RE BOTH AQUARIANS

ELIZABETH ALLEN

Kelly learns the real meaning of help through Camilla's problems.

The minute I got off the bus, my cousin ran up to me and before I could even say hello, grabbed hold of my new green coat by the collar.

"Groovy!" she shouted. Camilla is a shouter. "And I love that color! Am I glad we wear the same size!"

"No," I said, firmly. "No clothes swapping, Camilla."

I made the coat myself as a 4H project, and won a prize with it.

"Zodiac buttons." Camilla still wasn't noticing me, just my coat. "Fortunately, we were born under the same sign," she said contentedly.

"*No*," I repeated.

I'd sent in box tops from Wheat Zippies (one Zodiac button for each box top) until I had seven

Aquarius buttons. The buttons look just right on the coat, but I will never be able to look a Wheat Zippie in the face again.

"Camilla," I groaned, "you'll rip me to shreds!" She was actually trying to get the coat off me. "By the way, hello. *Greetings*."

"Hi yourself," said Camilla. "I suppose you *won't* let me wear it even once — you meanie."

Anything of mine, for some reason, has an absolute fascination for her. When we were six, she made such a fuss at a family reunion about wanting my new Barbie doll that I finally gave it to her. A few years later, she borrowed my tennis racket and left it out in the rain, and last Christmas she had managed to completely wreck my new typewriter.

"After all, we're both *Aquarians*," she said. "That ought to mean something."

"It's just that you're so rough on things," I explained.

"Oh, yes. The stupid typewriter," she said. "But Mom got you another one. After you ratted on me."

I *had* ratted on her. College was coming up, and I needed that typewriter. And besides, I will take just so much — from anybody.

"Well," Camilla said, brightly now, "since the opening hostilities are over, shall we go to the car?"

I giggled. Camilla does have a good sense of humor.

We made our way out of the bus station into the sharp spring air. Camilla and her parents come to us at Christmas, and occasionally some of us visit them. My aunt had invited me down for a few days during spring vacation, and I'd told my parents that I would go, but for a few days only. They knew that I am not too wild about Camilla, and so they had agreed to the two day limit. My parents are fairly good about letting me make my own decisions.

As we went on down the street I heard a voice behind us say, "Twins?"

Camilla and I are often taken for sisters and sometimes twins. Yet we are so different! We both have long brown hair with a reddish cast and green-gray eyes, but actually the resemblance is superficial. Camilla has a better figure — until recently, I had *no* figure — and I must admit that she is better looking than I am. She also has about three times as many clothes as I have. (That's why I was determined to hang on to my coat.)

"How've you been, Kelly?" she asked me now. "Still grabbing off A's, as usual?"

"I manage to keep the teachers fooled most of the time," I said. "How's the singing going?"

"Okay," said Camilla. "No offers from La Scala as yet."

Camilla really loves music and works hard at her vocal exercises.

We got to the car too soon; I was enjoying looking about at all the hustle and bustle of the city. Van Buren, where I live, is a small town in the fruit-belt part of the state. It's pretty. But when you've seen the one movie they show at the Rialto every week, that's it.

"Kelly," Camilla said as we took off, "I need your help. I have a problem."

Camilla always has a problem.

"Maybe you can make mother see that I've got

210

to go to Sommers College as planned," she sighed. "I'm just not the type for a big university."

I stopped trying to look into the windows of stores and turned to her.

"But you were all set for Sommers!" I was really surprised. At Christmas there had been great jubilation because Camilla had been accepted at this small college in a nearby state. In fact, there had been more comment about Camilla's acceptance at Sommers than there had been about the scholarship I'd been given from Beloit.

"Mom's goofing things up," Camilla groaned. "My grades improved a little after the pressure over college lessened, and now she's just determined that I go to State. She and Daddy went there."

Camilla's problems usually consisted of the fact that she had been scolded for not picking up her room, or that she was on foot because she'd gotten a traffic ticket, or that she had been grounded because she'd rolled in at 2:00 A.M. But now, for the first time, I felt that Camilla did have a problem.

"I think Sommers would be a lot better for you than State," I said.

"Tell Mom that for me, will you please?" Camilla sighed. "I need to get away from home. As far away as possible."

She did. Besides, her poor mother needed a rest. My aunt has tried and tried to shape her up, without much success.

"Sommers isn't so great academically — I mean, it's no Beloit — but it does have a good music department," Camilla said. "And they have this choral group that makes a tour every year," she added, eagerly. "Maybe I could be in it."

"Right," I said.

"I'm so dumb," Camilla wailed.

"You aren't dumb," I told her quickly. She's always had this idea that she was dumb. If Camilla could make some kind of real achievement in college, it would do worlds for her.

We drove into the suburbs toward the neat white colonial house which was her home.

"Kelly, dear!" My aunt swooped over me the moment we arrived. "What's this nonsense about your only staying until tomorrow?"

"I have to get back," I said firmly.

"Oh, all right, then. We're happy to have you for even a short visit. You're looking marvelous! And what a smashing coat!"

"She made it," Camilla said. "I don't see why they can't teach sewing at my stupid school. And green's my favorite color," she wailed. "But Kelly won't even let me try it on!"

There we were, back with the coat bit again.

"How nice everything looks!" I was trying to change the subject.

It did. Our house is apt to have one of my brother's baseball mitts on a chair, and my mother's choir music all over the piano, and for some reason my little sister's doll buggy is always in the hall.

Camilla is an only child.

I called my folks to tell them I'd arrived safely and went on upstairs to unpack. As I put away my things, I could hear Camilla and her mother arguing downstairs.

"That movie you want to go to is for 'mature' audiences," my aunt complained.

"I am considered very mature for my age!" Camilla shouted.

She sounded as though she were in kindergarten, and I couldn't help but giggle. And I thought, as I hung up my new coat, that people our age are always talking about how "mature" we are — but actually, few of us are really mature. How could we be? And then I stood there for a moment, staring at my coat. I called it my "good luck" coat because of the Aquarius buttons, and also because I was wearing it the day I'd heard about my scholarship. But, as my parents had pointed out, I'd gotten the scholarship because I'd worked hard all through high school (and I do "book" a lot; nothing comes easy). We make our own luck. I know that.

Camilla had to go to choir practice and my aunt had an errand, so we were soon off in the car which my aunt and Camilla share, with my cousin loudly complaining because she does not have her *very own car* (and frankly I am surprised that Camilla doesn't complain about not having her *very own jet*).

When we let Camilla off at the church, I decided to plunge right in with the favor my cousin had asked me to do her. It was one of the few sensible ideas she'd ever had.

"Don't you feel that a small college would be the best choice for Camilla?" I asked.

"In some ways, yes," my aunt said, frowning at the windshield. "And in some ways, no. College should offer a real challenge, *I* feel."

"I agree." I paused. "But college should give you a chance to — to develop any talent you have too. Camilla does have a good voice. And Sommers has a fine music department."

"Yes, but *Kelly*," Aunt sounded quite excited, "next year at State they'll have a voice coach who once worked at a European conservatory! Someone who has coached opera stars; think of it!"

You know that old expression, "My heart sank"? Well, of course no heart really sinks, but I felt myself more or less sinking all over. Camilla didn't really expect to be an opera star. She just wanted to do the best she could. She wanted to sing in a chorus.

"Think of it!" my aunt repeated.

I hesitated, because it was fairly apparent that Camilla was doomed to go to State no matter what I said. But I did point out that as a freshman she probably wouldn't have a chance at this coach, and at Sommers she could be in on all the musical affairs. My aunt listened to me politely, but I had the feeling that I was making no headway.

"And then, State's so *close*," she said. "I can run over and help Camilla if she gets in any kind of jam. That's something you just wouldn't understand, Kelly; you never seem to need any help."

I was so startled I couldn't think of anything to say for a moment. I've had a lot of help. It was my mother who really taught me to sew, and my dad spent I don't know how many Sunday afternoons patiently letting me drive him on every back road around Van Buren, so that I could get my license.

My aunt glanced over and flashed me a smile.

"Aquarius buttons!" she said. "Isn't it weird, this new interest in astrology?"

"Yes." I was glad we were off on another subject, and I've always enjoyed discussing things with my aunt. "Yet I was thinking, today . . . we have to make our own luck. Or try to."

She nodded.

"'The fault, dear Brutus, lies not in our stars,
But in ourselves, that we are underlings.'"

"Right!" I said. "That's from *Julius Caesar,* isn't it?"

In some ways my aunt is just terrific. I mean, there are not too many people who can pull out a Shakespearian quotation like that.

We stopped at a store for a moment and then picked up Camilla, who was so pleased with the way a cantata was going that she was very agreeable on the way home. But the minute we got in the house another argument started. My aunt wanted my uncle to take us all out to a club for dinner, and Camilla insisted that this would make us late for our dates. Camilla lost the argument, and retreated upstairs in a huff to wash her hair.

"Camilla, please don't wash your hair!" called my aunt. "It won't dry in time, and you'll catch cold. . . ."

"Stupid old club," Camilla was muttering, when I got upstairs. (I had stayed in the living room a few minutes to talk to my aunt and try to calm her down.) "Stupid, stupid, stupid!"

She had finished her shampoo and was rolling up her hair — using, I noticed, my curlers.

"Camilla," I moaned. "Can't you stay out of my things?"

"Well, your curlers are bigger than mine, Kelly. Where did you get them, anyway?"

"You might try that little specialty store called Woolworth's," I said.

"I suppose you're wearing your peach knit." Camilla was looking thoughtful, and had of course ignored my weak attempt at humor. "I was just looking through your clothes. . . ."

"I'm sure you were."

"And since *I'm* wearing this green and gold plaid, I thought—"

"No," I repeated. "I will *not* lend you my green coat."

"Are you sure you weren't born under the sign of Taurus?" she asked. "Boy, are you stubborn."

She crawled under her hair dryer, which is, incidentally, a full-size one.

"You can wear anything of mine," she said. "If—"

"No," I repeated.

Camilla is the one who should have been born under the sign of the bull.

But by the time we got around to dressing, we were again trying to carry on a sensible conversation. She asked me if I'd had any luck on the college situation, and I told her I'd tried, and would make another stab at it. She thanked me. This college bit was really important to her.

My uncle arrived and we went to the club, which is a lovely place with delicious food. But it's a very leisurely sort of setup. As the meal dragged on, I realized that Camilla was getting restless.

"Mom, I told you that these boys were coming at eight," she said. "And they won't even be able to get into the house."

"I will not be rushed," said my aunt. "We all

216

hurry too much." She proceeded to take her time over deciding on her dessert, and would have had a brandy later, except that my uncle overruled her.

Sure enough, a car was leaving just as we went into the driveway. But a voice called out to Camilla and soon I saw the car turn and start back; we would be going out after all.

"Mom just never listens," Camilla said bewilderedly as we rushed into the house and tore upstairs. "I told her way back last week that I had a date for tonight, and that I'd get a boy for you, and we'd double."

It did seem strange to me that my aunt had more or less ignored her daughter's plans. There had always been friction between these two, but I'd always thought that this was entirely Camilla's fault. Now I wasn't so sure.

"You'll like Cleet," Camilla said, whacking away at her hair. "He's very dynamic — Scorpio, you know."

Cleet. If it was Cleet Townley, I knew I'd like him, because I had met him once before and liked him. But I hadn't registered at all with Cleet, although I'd spent an entire evening with him.

Then I noticed something. We were in Camilla's tiny dressing room, which she had brightened up considerably by painting pink and orange poppies all over the walls.

"What happened to your flowers?" I gasped. They were gone.

"Mom had them covered with wallpaper," Camilla said in an odd, flat voice. "She insisted that they didn't match the rest of the house." Her face, as she turned toward me, had a snuffed-out look.

"They were beautiful," I said. "They were yours."

"Never mind that now, Kelly. About Cleet; he's going to Beloit too, and he sails, and he works weekends in a gas station. Got it?"

I forgot about the poppies and nodded, sort of numbly. I am no stand-out in the dating department. Oh, I go out. In fact, I've gone out quite a bit this year. But I still have this funny feeling just before a date: I'd like to leave, immediately, for points unknown. I freeze.

"Relax," Camilla hissed at me as we went downstairs. "You look great."

Maybe, I thought, tonight would be different. *I had on my good luck coat.*

My aunt was talking on the phone, and the two boys were sitting rather stiffly in the living room, chatting with my uncle, *waiting*, something I know boys were sitting rather stiffly in the living room, one of them was Cleet Townley, all right, just as I remembered him. I don't know whether you'd call him handsome or not — his hair is dark and his features are strong — but I liked his face.

My uncle tactfully melted off somewhere.

"Are you Kelly?" Cleet said.

"The same." I smiled at him. All my going-to-points-unknown feeling had stopped.

"But you're a skinny little kid with freckles. And you squeal in all the wrong places at the movies."

"Little kids grow up, Cleet," I told him. "And I do *not* squeal at movies."

"We'd better split," Camilla's date called to us at the door. "If we don't hurry the last show will start."

Well, it was one of those evenings when every-thing went along just about right. Ronnie, Camilla's date, drove, which gave me more of a chance to get reacquainted with Cleet.

"Camilla tells me you're going to Beloit too," I said.

"University of Wisconsin," he sighed. "Oh, well, she at least got the right state; pretty good for Camilla."

"I heard that!" Camilla shouted from the front seat. "I'm through with you, Cleet Townley. You can have him, Kelly."

"Fine," I said.

"It's always nice to be asked," Cleet groaned.

He didn't seem to mind being kidded or anything, and pretty soon we were talking about school, and he was telling me about his gas station job, and I was telling him various things I do.

It is really a good idea to meet people from dif-ferent places. I've always had this fixed notion that "city" people were different from "small town" people — spoiled and so on. That's silly.

Anyway, we all had a good time. I couldn't even tell you what the movie was about now, but I had a good time. Afterward we went to one of those pizza places and Mama Cass was singing on the juke box and Camilla said poo, she could sing louder than that, and proceeded to practice her scales. It turned out that Cleet's family had a cottage on Maple Leaf Lake, which is not too far from Four Mile, where our cottage is, and that we both sailed Lightning class.

"I will definitely see you on some lake or other, Kelly," Cleet said, as we went back to the car. "And what's this about you leaving *tomorrow?*"

"Well, yes, I am." I was regretting that.

"It's all right. There are such things as telephones," he told me. "And I might even have to come up your way soon to check out the cottage. I want to be sure it's ready for summer." I nodded. The summer was starting to look interesting.

He wrote down my phone number and my address later, and by the time we got back to my aunt and uncle's I was on that well-known cloud nine. I didn't even mind that my aunt had waited up for us, although I thought it a little strange. My folks don't wait up for me.

Of course the boys just took off. My aunt wanted to hear all about our evening, and what movie we had seen, and what we had done afterward, and how I'd gotten along with Cleet. It was just as though we were in junior high. It was weird.

"Let's have some hot chocolate and *talk!*" she said, enthusiastically.

"You have the hot chocolate," said Camilla. "I'm going to bed."

I've always thought Camilla was rude to her mother, but the hot chocolate talk idea didn't appeal to me either. Not at all.

"Kelly," my aunt said, when we were alone in the kitchen. Her face was tired. "You see how it is? No communication."

"Oh, Camilla was just sleepy, perhaps."

"She never wants to talk to me." My aunt sounded really unhappy. "I'd give anything if she would."

She never wants to talk to me. But what had Camilla said? "Mom never listens."

"Kelly, *you,* as a dear relative and yet outside

our immediate family circle, can perhaps see things I don't," she said. "What do I do with Camilla that is so wrong?"

"Well —" and I almost said, "You treat her as though she's a little kid, and so she acts like one." But I didn't. I just couldn't say that. And I was thinking too of those papered-over poppies. I didn't know what to say about the poppies. I hesitated.

"Kelly, I am serious," my aunt said.

And she did seem to be serious. That's what threw me off.

"You mentioned earlier that you felt Camilla should go to Sommers, a little jackrabbit college nobody ever heard of," she added disgustedly. "Do you honestly feel that this is a good plan?"

"Yes. I —"

"Because I want only what is best for Camilla," she said. "And I still feel that she should go to a good university."

"She'd be *lost* at State." I hadn't meant to say it quite so loudly. "The classes are so big, and the competition's so fierce —"

"But she'd be so close that I could help her," my aunt interrupted. "She could either come home weekends, or I'd go over there. I'd be able to supervise everything. And it would be such fun to have an excuse to scurry over there occasionally!"

"Look here," I said. "You've *been* to college. This is Camilla's turn."

I should never have said it. I shouldn't have been so harsh. I should have kept quiet.

"What!" she gasped, and her face went as white and taut as a sheet on a line. "What do you *mean* by saying that?"

221

"I'm sorry if I hurt your feelings." I was horrified at myself, and all I could think of was how I could apologize. "I — I know that you have given a lot of thought to Camilla's education. And I know that you could help her and all, as you say. But we — we must develop our own strengths." This was, I now realized, what my family had let me do. They'd helped me when I needed help, but they had also let me to my own way.

"You make me feel as though I'm some sort of monster, Kelly."

My aunt's voice was cold. She was still mad, and I guess the more she thought about what I'd said, the madder she got.

"You nasty little *snip!*" she glared.

"That's enough."

It was my uncle, standing in the doorway. I hadn't even known he was there.

"Kelly is a guest in our home," he said. "And I consider this conversation most unfortunate. Also, as it is late, I suggest we all retire." I was ready to.

I said good night, mentioned that I'd be leaving in the morning — I'd made a quick decision to take an early bus — and went upstairs. But although I went to bed, they didn't. They had an argument. In fact, it sounded more like a big fat fight. I didn't know what it was about and I didn't want to know.

I got up early and dressed and packed. Originally I'd planned on a little shopping and seeing an exhibit in a museum, but all I could think of now was getting away.

I put on my coat and went downstairs with my suitcase to call a taxi.

There was Camilla's father, waiting for me. He

didn't look as though he'd had much sleep, and he is a rather shadowy-appearing person anyhow. He looked gray. I felt sorry for him.

"I'll drive you to the bus station, Kelly," he said. "Would you like some coffee?"

"No, thanks. I — I appreciate your getting up. You needn't have."

"I wanted to. You brought something to a boil that's been simmering a long time, Kelly. And incidentally, Camilla is going to go to the college of her choice, not her mother's choice."

So that was what the fight had been about. "I'm glad," I said.

"And please don't misjudge your aunt. She really has wanted the best for Camilla, and she does love her daughter."

She does love her daughter. Yes, I knew she did. But I'm not sure that love — that *kind* of love — had been enough for Camilla. She needed respect as well as love. I didn't say that. I'd already said too much.

"I'll get the car, Kelly."

"All right," I managed a smile. "But just a moment. I want to write a note."

"If it's to your aunt, I really don't believe that this is necessary. And I do hope we can forget all this unpleasantness."

"I hope so too," I said. "But actually, I wanted to write a note to Camilla."

He looked pleased, and nodded. I rushed upstairs, but I didn't write the note after all. I went to Camilla's room and paused, and looked down at her. She was asleep, looking younger than my little sister. And yet her face, in repose, was sad.

We do make our own luck, I thought. But for some people, imprisoned and . . . *snuffed*, their luck is poor. Their luck is terrible.

No wonder Camilla had always wanted to use my things. But what I had she could not borrow, and I could not lend.

I took off my new green coat with the Aquarius buttons. After all, my uncle's car was heated, and so was the bus. I put the coat on a chair, where Camilla would see it the very first thing when she woke up, and know I'd given it to her.

She needed it. I didn't.